IT'S ALWAYS ᴛʜᴇ HUSBAND

A Hope Ridge Thriller

ROSEMARY WILLHIDE

SMALL TOWN MYSTERIES

IT'S ALWAYS THE HUSBAND
A Hope Ridge Thriller
Copyright © SEPTEMBER 2023 ROSEMARY WILLHIDE
Paperback ISBN: 979-8-861340-13-7

Cover Art by Poppy Designs

ALL RIGHTS RESERVED

Dateline ™	*Ring* ™	*Louis Vuitton* ™
Lululemon ™	*Ping* ™	*Cheerios* ™
Botox ™	*Oxycodone* ™	*Amazon* ™
Instagram ™	*Tito's* ™	*Visine* ™
TikTok ™	*Altoids* ™	*Café du Monde* ™
Facebook ™	*Heinz 57* ™	*Google* ™
Pottery Barn ™	*Venmo* ™	*iPad* ™
Netflix ™	*Uber* ™	*Pinterest* ™
Bravo ™	*Gucci* ™	*Prada* ™
Discovery ™		

DEDICATION

THIS BOOK IS FOR THE husbands, the good ones that buy their wives books, not the "murdery" ones. LOL!

Two of the best husbands I know are my husband, Bill Johnson, and my dad, Charlie Willhide. Thank you for being amazing men, I love you both so much. Cheers to the good ones! This book is for you!

QUOTE

What we do in the dark will eventually come to light.

The day before Thanksgiving

This is how it's going to end for me. This is how I die. I'm completely pinned down. I'm immobile. Even if I were stronger, I wouldn't fight. I have no fight left in me. The grip around my throat is tightening, squeezing the life out of me. I'm gasping as I draw my last few breaths. Maybe I deserve this. All the lies, the secrets, the pretending, it's over now. I resign myself and let go.

Dead…

CHAPTER ONE

Six weeks earlier

Bella Wright

"HEY, I THOUGHT YOU WERE coming to bed," my husband said as he crept up behind me.

I flinched and my fingers froze over the keyboard of my laptop. "Jack! You scared the crap out of me."

He joined me on the sofa. "Sorry, love. So, what's the latest mystery that you're working on?"

"Something from our old neighborhood. I've gotten a little obsessed. I think I'm about seventy percent sure who did it."

True crime blogs were my drug. I considered myself an amateur detective and relished watching for updates on cold cases. Whether it was a missing person or an unsolved homicide, connecting the dots that led to closure was a high like no other. As a mostly silent observer, I hadn't personally contributed to any arrests, but I was getting better at looking at the pieces of the puzzle. One of these days I was going to solve a whodunit and start a blog of my own.

"Our old neighborhood is in our rearview mirror for a reason." Jack sighed. "I thought we agreed to move on. Why don't you come to bed?"

I hadn't agreed to anything. "Okay. I just need five more minutes."

"Mrs. Wright… I insist."

I broke out in gooseflesh when he called me Mrs. Wright. It was his way of saying he wanted me. We'd been married fifteen years, and if he still found my forty-two-year-old ass desirable, who was I to deny him?

I shot him a sideways glance and grinned. "Well, since you insisted, Mister Wright."

I signed off and mumbled under my breath, "Bella W, out."

When I tossed my laptop to the side, his bright, blue eyes sparkled, and he gathered me into his arms. "You know we haven't christened all the rooms in our new house."

I tore off my long-sleeved T-shirt, relieved I had on my date night bra. "What did you have in mind?"

He rose and unzipped his jeans. "You and me up against the big, bay window. Let's put on an X-rated show for the entire neighborhood."

I chuckled, darted to the wooden shutters, and closed them. "Jack, that's not fair. You're in DC working during the week. I'm the one that'll have to face these people Monday through Friday."

My husband was a successful commercial contractor and got an offer he couldn't refuse in DC. Rather than living close to another big city, we decided on a small town in Pennsylvania, and he would commute. Eventually, he hoped to make it a four-day work week, but so far that hadn't happened.

For now, it was cool, since I'd been busting my butt getting our new house in Hope Ridge organized. I unpacked the last box on Friday and enjoyed this glorious weekend with the love of my life. Hopefully, once he got more settled, we'd be enjoying three-day weekends together.

With care, he placed my laptop on the coffee table and opened his arms to me. "Then let's do it on the sofa like we used to when we first met. Remember the olive green, velvet porn couch from my first apartment?"

"How could I forget? We defiled it. It probably had more bodily fluid on it than a crime scene."

He stripped down to his boxer briefs. "You want to relive the glory days?"

His body still looked the same as it did in his thirties. With his long, lean runner's physique, Jack was fine as hell at forty-five.

I licked my lips. "Of course I do, but that is a brand spanking new ten-thousand-dollar custom-made couch."

Jack tossed the plush throw on it and took a seat. "Hmm... did you say spanking?"

"You're so bad and irresistible."

In the sexiest walk I could muster, I sauntered toward him, removed the rest of my clothes, and straddled my hot husband.

He ran his fingers through my hair. "Hmm... you look gorgeous as a redhead. I'm loving it."

"Are you sure it isn't too short?"

"No. It's sexy as hell."

With that, he kissed my neck and I turned into a puddle of goo. Jack knew all of my pleasure triggers. As he took off my bra and caressed my breast, I gripped his broad shoulders and let out a moan.

"Let's take this upstairs," he whispered. "I have to have you, baby."

As he whisked me up to the primary bedroom in our beautiful home, I thought it couldn't get any better than this. I had the best husband in the entire world. How did I get so lucky?

IN THE AFTERMATH, TANGLED IN the sheets, I exhaled. "You still got it, Mister Wright."

"That's all you, gorgeous."

"I wish we could stay like this forever."

His lips grazed my temple. "I do too. Unfortunately, four a.m. comes early."

I squeezed him tighter. "Would it be so terrible if you stayed here with me?"

He chuckled. "You've said that every Sunday night since we moved."

"I know. I'm going to miss you."

"I'll miss you too, but I always come back to you. Maybe this week I'll leave DC early Thursday morning. We'll have a three-day weekend."

"Don't tease me."

He threw back the sheet and sat up. "I'm not. I'm going to figure it out. In the meantime, maybe get out of the house a little. Go meet the neighbors."

My eyelids grew heavy. "People are overrated," I muttered.

"Maybe a little human interaction would do you some good. You can't live on a steady diet of true crime blogs."

"I don't. I also listen to true crime podcasts and watch Dateline."

"Think about it," Jack said and got out of bed.

When he pulled out his suitcase, I whined, "Less packing, more cuddling."

He grinned, came to me, and kissed my forehead. "It's late. Get some rest. This week will fly by. I'll see you again before you know it."

"You promise?"

"Yeah, I promise. I love you."

I forced myself to stay awake so I could nestle in close when he came back to bed. With a yawn, I said, "Make sure you kiss me goodbye before you leave in the morning, even if I'm asleep."

"I don't want to disturb you, sweetie."

"Disturb me, please. I don't want to miss a single kiss from my amazing husband. I insist, Mister Wright."

"Whatever you say, Mrs. Wright. And remember, I'll always come home to you."

CHAPTER TWO

"HI. UH... CAN I HELP you?" I asked the pretty blonde woman on my porch holding a basket.

"Oh... um... I'm your neighbor, Nicole, from across the street."

"Nice to meet you. I'm Bella... well, Annabelle. My friends call me Bella."

"Well, Bella, I wanted to welcome you to the neighborhood."

"That's so sweet. I just made some coffee. Do you want to come in?"

She smiled and handed me the basket. "Sure. That would be great. They'll go great with the blueberry muffins."

"Follow me to the kitchen," I said and led the way.

"Awesome sauce. Wow! You look all moved in. How are you enjoying living in The Heights?"

"I haven't had a chance to explore it much, but so far so good."

Under the bright, overhead light of the kitchen, Nicole seemed familiar. Or maybe it was because she resembled every over-forty mom in my last neighborhood. The perfectly manicured nails, the Lululemon yoga outfit with matching hoodie, the forehead that didn't budge, and sadness disguised with a smile. I'd seen this before and as a rule, I never got too close, but Nicole seemed to have an extra dash of charm. Maybe she would be an exception.

I gestured to one of the chairs surrounding our oversized kitchen island. "Have a seat. I'll fetch you some coffee."

When she sat, Nicole asked, "I'd love a latte if you can swing it?"

"Uh... how about some pumpkin spice creamer? I heard it was good."

"That sounds super. So, do you have kids? I haven't seen any cars in your driveway."

"Uh... we don't."

"Why not?"

"Um... it kind of never worked out for Jack and me."

"Well, you look young. There's still time for babies. Don't you think?"

As I sat down our tray with coffee, napkins and plates, I replied, "No. I don't like kids."

Her jaw went slack. "You don't like what?"

"Kids. They seem kind of annoying," I said in a half-joking tone.

Of course, Jack and I wanted children. We agonized about not being able to conceive. To avoid further discussion about my infertility issues, I would try to make light of our childless household and not answer any more questions.

Nicole let out an uncomfortable laugh. "You know what? I have two daughters and they are kind of annoying. You might be the smart one."

I joined her at the table. "How old are they?"

She beamed at the chance to talk about them. "Oh, Emily is my oldest. She's twenty-one and Sarah just turned nineteen."

"Stop! There's no way you're old enough to have a twenty-one-year-old."

"I am. It's called Botox. I'm going to turn forty-eight next month, but the other ladies in the neighborhood think I'm still thirty-nine and I don't correct them."

I popped a piece of blueberry muffin in my mouth. "It'll be our secret. Mmm... these are good."

"Thanks. I got them on Main Street at the cutest bakery. Have you been?"

"On Main Street? No. But I hear it's lovely."

"Hope Ridge is very quaint and friendly. The families in the neighborhood spend most of their time at the Country Club. You know, golf and tennis. Now that it's fall there are a lot of theme nights at the club, and of course lots of house parties. Oh! You should come to my Wine Down Wednesday this week and meet everyone."

"That sounds wonderful. I might take you up on that?"

"Great. So, what does your husband do?"

"He's a commercial contractor in DC. He got an offer he couldn't pass up, so we picked up and moved. Jack stays there during the week and comes home on the weekends."

Her eyes grew wide with dollar signs. She knew being a commercial contractor in DC meant we weren't hurting for money. "Wow! Where did you move from?"

"Chicago. Well, the suburbs. Do you know Chicago?"

"No. I don't. We relocated from Pi... Pine Hills. It's not too far from here. My husband, Dave, is a realtor and since Hope Ridge is thriving it seemed like a perfect spot to settle down."

"I got a great deal on this house. It was below the asking price. We were amazed."

She nodded and sipped her coffee as if she knew a juicy secret. "Yeah, it's been empty for a while."

"Interesting. So, your daughters, are they in college?"

"No. Emily has some issues with anxiety and depression. She felt like going to college would be a waste of time, so she's trying to find her thing. And Sarah, she's taking a gap year and deciding what she wants to do."

"Real-life work experience is nothing to sneeze at. I have a degree in philosophy and English which means I'm qualified to do... hmm... I haven't figured that out yet."

She leaned forward. "So, no kids, you don't work, and your husband is in DC part of the week. How do you fill all your time? Are you like . . . an undercover spy?"

A polite chuckle escaped. "Um... just a few hobbies. Lately moving took up most of my time. So, how long have you lived in The Heights?"

"We're coming up on our second anniversary right around my birthday next month. Dave and I absolutely adore it, but the girls think it's boring. I tell them if you're that bored get a job."

"What do they do with their time?"

"Instagram mostly. Also, TikTok, but not Facebook, because apparently, that's for old people like us."

"Do they want to be influencers? I hear that's like a thing now."

She whipped her phone out from the pocket of her jacket. "Here, I'll show you the girls. Sarah loves makeup and does tutorials."

As I watched her video, Nicole kept talking. "She favors me. Don't you think?"

"Yeah, the blonde hair and the exact same smile. She's very pretty."

Once the video wrapped up, she kept scrolling. "Now this is my other daughter, Emily. She's a little more camera shy and mostly posts sarcastic memes."

Emily was much less vivacious than Sarah. In the photo, she looked like Eeyore with unkempt, long, brown hair.

"She is quite attractive too," I commented.

"Oh, that's so sweet of you to say. Emily gained the freshman fifteen without going to college. She used to play sports and then we moved a couple of times, and she became more withdrawn. I honestly don't know what's going to become of her."

The expression on Nicole's face grew so grim, Botox couldn't mask it. It looked like a horrible memory flashed in her head, but she caught herself quickly and plastered on a smile. "Oh, uh... are you on the gram? I'll follow you. What's your last name?"

"It's Wright, but I'm not on social media."

"Not even Facebook?" she asked in shock.

"No. I don't see the point. My husband and I are pretty private, so it doesn't make sense for us."

"Huh... now I'm convinced you're a secret agent or something."

"What can I say, I'm just a dull housewife."

"Definitely not dull. I hope you'll come over on Wednesday and meet my friends. I think you'd enjoy yourself."

"Who would I be meeting?"

"Well, there's Wendy Anderson. Sometimes she's kind of in a funk because she thinks her husband is cheating on her.

"Is he?"

"I mean, probably. Lance is impossibly handsome and has been known to have a wandering eye. And there's Julie Mitchell. She's kind of shy at first, but after some wine, she loosens up and will talk your ear off about her favorite subject, which is herself. Julie is a single mom who moved to the neighborhood right before we did. She took her ex to the cleaners in their divorce settlement. And Catherine Myers is a total hoot. She and her husband, Mick, work with my husband. They're realtors too. You've probably seen their billboards for 'Love it or List it.' That's their agency."

"I like the title. It's catchy."

"Thank you! I'm the one that came up with it. They were going to call it The Agency or something like that. For once, someone listened to me."

I sipped my coffee. "How long have you two been married?"

"Oh, gosh, it feels like forever. What about you?"

"Same. Oh... I didn't catch your last name."

She cleared her throat. "Uh... it's Taylor. If you change your mind and join Instagram, I'm under Nicole Taylor HIB.

"What's HIB?"

"Head bitch in charge." She clicked her tongue. "It's kind of an inside joke between me and my husband."

"I love it. A strong woman who rules the roost."

"Sure. Something like that. You know, I should go and let you get your day started. So what do you think? My place, Wednesday night at seven?"

"Yeah, I'd love to meet everyone. You've painted quite a colorful picture."

She rose from her chair. "Awesome sauce."

As I walked her out, I asked, "What can I bring?"

"Uh, nothing. Unless you don't like wine."

"I love wine," I fibbed. I didn't drink much. I preferred to remain in total control. "Maybe I'll head into town and pick up something from the bakery. I can't come empty handed."

"Suit yourself," Nicole said with glee as she left. "See you then."

After I shut the door, I went to the bay window, peeked out the shutters, and watched her walk across the street. She was hustling.

With my curiosity bubbling, I made a list of the neighbors' names in my notebook and opened up my laptop.

"Let's see who I'm dealing with," I mumbled to myself.

I began with Nicole Taylor. Why did I have an inkling there was more to her than meets the eye?

CHAPTER THREE

Wednesday evening

"BELLA!" NICOLE SQUEALED. "I WAS beginning to give up on you. Come on in."

As I crossed the threshold of her home the scent of pumpkin spice smacked me in the face. It was next-level and almost nauseating.

"Your home is gorgeous!" I said as I followed her across the hardwood floor and down the hallway. By gorgeous, I meant enormous. It was more modern than our place, very Pottery Barn, with no personality or personal touches.

"Thank you. And thanks for bringing ice. I always run out."

"I also have some double chocolate brownies from the bakery you told me about."

When we landed in the kitchen, she took the brownies from me, and I placed the bag of ice on the counter while laughter sounded in the other room.

"You must have quite the crowd for Wine Down Wednesday."

She giggled. "Catherine has been cracking us up all night. I guess Mia caught wind of our get-together and invited herself, or Catherine did and won't fess up to it."

"Who's Mia? I don't remember a Mia."

"Oh, you'll see," she replied and arranged the brownies on a plate.

"Nicole, we need more Chardonnay," a husky female voice called.

"Coming right up," Nicole replied and headed to the fridge. "Oh, uh, would you mind putting the ice in the freezer for me? I'll just be a second." She pulled out the wine and raised it in the air. "Hostess duty calls."

Left alone in her kitchen, I plopped down my purse by the stack of mail, picked up the ice, and opened the freezer. It was full.

Hmm… she probably had a freezer in the garage. In our old neighborhood, any mom with more than one kid had a freezer in the garage. Taking a guess, I opened up a door. Bingo. It led into their three-car garage, and they had a freezer out there. When I lifted the lid and set it inside, I turned and noticed one of the cars was covered. Maybe it was an expensive sports car.

My nosiness got the best of me and I peeled back the black covering on the passenger's side, but all I saw was extensive damage right above the front tire. It wasn't a fancy car at all. It was a hunter-green sedan that had obviously been in an accident. *How odd*, I thought as I put the cover back on and stepped away from the car.

"Who the hell are you?" a male voice grumbled.

Shaken, I gasped. "Oh… hi… uh… I'm your new neighbor from across the street, Bella. You must be, Dave?"

His icy stare practically pinned me to the wall. "What are you doing out here? The party's in the back room."

Dave stood well over six feet and had to weigh more than two hundred pounds. His intimidating demeanor wasn't what I pictured when Nicole told me about her husband, the real estate agent.

"I'm so sorry," I replied. "I brought some ice and there wasn't any room in your freezer, so I thought maybe you had one in your garage. Um… so… yeah… that's pretty much it."

He relaxed his firm stance. "Okay. The freezer in the kitchen is always full. There's never any room. Let me show you where the ladies are hanging out."

With tentative steps, I followed him. It was as if I'd just left the principal's office. "Thanks, I appreciate it."

Once we were back in the kitchen, Emily, who I recognized from her photo, huffed at Dave. "Dad, Mom says I can't have any wine, but I'm twenty-one and I say that's crap."

He ran his hand through his thick, light brown hair. "Didn't one of the ladies bring hot chocolate?"

"Uh… hello… I'm not ten," she snipped.

Emily had a permanent scowl etched on her face and was almost as tall as her dad. Perhaps Dave had a soft spot for his oldest daughter, because he grabbed a glass and poured her some wine from an already opened bottle of red. "Take this and head to your room. And please, don't tell your sister you have it. She's still underage."

A near smile emerged. "Thanks, Dad."

"By the way, this is Bella, our new neighbor across the street," he said.

"Nice to meet you, Emily."

"How do you know my name?" she asked and made a sour face.

"Your mom came over and showed me your picture from Instagram."

"Whatever," she replied and snatched up her glass of wine.

"Do you have kids?" Dave inquired after Emily left the kitchen.

"No. We don't."

"Consider yourself lucky. I only have two and they're a handful. They fight and they never seem to have enough. Nicole raised two entitled brats."

As inquisitive as I was about people, this was more information than I expected or wanted. While my initial search of Nicole and her family didn't prove fruitful, my gut said there was something going on in this grand house.

His cheeks turned red as he ranted some more and grabbed a beer. "The cackle fest is to your left. Welcome to the neighborhood."

When he left me on my own in the kitchen, I took a second to collect myself, wishing I had stayed home.

"Okay, Bella, you can do this. Plaster on a fake smile, stay twenty minutes, and then head to your sanctuary of true crime." Maybe there's a good serial killer documentary on Netflix to take my mind off of my conversation with Dave?

CHAPTER FOUR

"THERE YOU ARE," NICOLE EXCLAIMED. "I thought you got lost in the kitchen. Everyone, this is our new neighbor, Annabelle Wright. Her friends call her Bella."

A chorus of "hellos" and "welcomes" greeted me, while my cheeks flushed. With all eyes glued to me, this was more overwhelming than I anticipated.

"Let's get you a drink," the one and only brunette said and poured white wine into a glass and handed it to me. "I'm Catherine. I work in the real estate trenches with Nicole's husband, Dave. What do you do?"

"Um, at the moment, nothing. Uh… my husband, Jack, is a commercial contractor in DC. I guess I'm just a boring housewife."

"There's no such thing," Catherine replied. "I'm not sure if Nicole told you who is who, but Julie, the blonde over there will talk your ear off in about two more drinks, and it will be all about her, if you know what I mean. And Wendy, the other blonde will probably start crying in twenty minutes."

"Is she okay?" I asked.

Catherine shrugged. "Who knows. Now, just to be a bitch, I'm the one that invited the gorgeous, tall bombshell, Mia. That can be our little secret."

Secrets seemed to run rampant in this charming, little neighborhood, The Heights. Mia grazed the buffet table on her own and I did wonder why this sexpot in the tight sweater dress with cascading, jet-black, straight hair was here. She was at least fifteen years younger than the soccer moms and appeared not to give any fucks. I had to know her story.

"Your secret is safe with me," I replied. "So, what's Mia's deal? She's like a diamond in a room full of cubic zirconia, no offense."

Catherine let out a loud boisterous laugh. "None taken. I like you already, Bella. So, Mia is married to none other than Samuel Wallace, a direct descendant of John Wallace, who is legendary around these parts. They have old, family money and Samuel is about as ancient as they come. I heard Mia was his caretaker and now she's his wife."

"Exactly how old is her husband, Samuel?"

"Older than dirt," she cackled. "Seriously, if you ever meet him, you'll think he's getting a head start on his dirt nap. I figured the poor girl needed a night out, so I extended the invite. Nicole is probably going to kill me later, but it was worth it to see the look on her face when Mia showed up."

As I made my rounds, meeting all the ladies, I noticed Nicole was the head bitch in charge. She had a certain charisma and knew how to command the room. Wendy and Julie hung on to every word she said. The three of them even had the exact same hair style, shoulder-length blonde hair with a few lowlights for contrast and no bangs to showcase their frozen foreheads.

My tousled, red bob, Mia's shiny, black locks, and Catherine's tasteful short brunette hairdo were out of step with the blondes.

"So, are you married?" Wendy Anderson asked in a quiet, yet friendly tone. She seemed to be the shyest of the blondes. "I mean, you're so pretty. My husband Lance always said he had a thing for redheads."

"Yes, I am. My husband's name is Jack. He works in DC during the week."

"Do you have kids?"

"No. It's just us."

If Wendy could've furrowed her brow she would've. "Huh… do you work?"

"Not at the moment. It sounds kind of silly, but I'm obsessed with true crime. You know, blogs, podcasts,

Dateline, stuff like that. I suppose if I had gotten serious about a career, I would've been a detective."

Wendy clasped my elbow and pulled me away from the other women. "Um, if I asked you to look into something, could you? I'd pay you for your time."

"Hmm... I don't know. I guess it depends on what it is. I couldn't do anything illegal."

Her hazel eyes welled up with tears. "I understand. My husband is a therapist and he's so wonderful... it's just... sometimes I wonder if he might be having an affair. I volunteer at my son's school, and I'm the assistant coach for his soccer and baseball teams. I don't have access to a lot of funds on the down-low, so I can't pay a private investigator. I looked into it. It's too expensive for me. Lance would notice if I spent that kind of money. But, if you did it, I could pay a little at a time. I'm sorry. I'm probably making you uncomfortable. This wine is going right to my head."

"No, you're not," I replied with genuine sympathy. "I would like to help you. Maybe stop by the house sometime next week and give me some information. I'll see what I can do."

"Thank you. Nicole is always telling me to buck up and not make waves. Julie tries to distract me by talking about the *Real Housewives* on Bravo. It's our guilty pleasure."

"We all need those."

"Do you watch Bravo?"

"No. But it sounds like I should. I mostly watch Dateline and Investigation Discovery. Stuff like that."

"Oh yeah. I get into a little true crime too. Lance calls them my murder shows."

"My husband Jack says the same thing."

Wendy exhaled. "I'm so glad you came tonight. You're a breath of fresh air."

Before I could respond Dave tromped into the room with a grim expression. "Ladies, I'm afraid we're going to have to call it a night."

Nicole took a few steps in Dave's direction. "What's wrong?"

"It's Emily and Sarah. They're both really sick," Dave replied. "I don't know if it's a bug or something they ate, but I think it might be best if everyone went home."

Catherine set down her wine glass. "Of course. Nicole, go be with your girls. I'll see everyone out."

While everyone gathered their things, Nicole rushed off and Dave followed. I stopped in the kitchen to pick up my bag and caught up to the ladies on the porch.

Catherine gave each of us a hug and sent us on our way. As I crossed the street, I realized Mia was right behind me, so I stopped.

"Hey, I'm sorry we didn't get to chat more," I said.

"That's okay. I figured you were like all the rest and didn't want to talk to me."

"Oh, no. That's not true. I would love to get to know you better."

"You mean that?"

"Of course. I'll be honest, I was kind of intimidated to talk to you. You're so gorgeous and you seem super cool. I'm kind of a nerd, and awkward at social gatherings."

Mia tilted her head as if she was trying to figure me out. "So, you're not like the blonde trio in there?"

"No. For what it's worth, I just moved here and don't know anyone. I barely even said two words to Julie. Now I'm wondering if she's feeling some type of way about me."

"From what I've observed, she probably didn't even notice. Julie is into Julie."

"Oh, I guess there's a lot to learn about this neighborhood. I could... I could use a friend."

Her demeanor softened. "I could too. I know what people say about me. They call me a gold digger, among other things. Catherine is the only person who has ever given me the time of day. I usually get judged before anyone gets to know me."

"If you ask me, they're probably a little jealous. It's a shame about Nicole's daughters, though. I wonder what made them sick."

"I don't know, but before you got there, I saw both of them eating all the sliders I brought. I got them from Bennie's food truck. It was in the neighborhood, parked by a house that's being renovated. Oh, great, I'll probably get the blame. That's all I need."

"It could've been anything. I remember when I was their age, I ate anything that wasn't nailed down."

"I still do," she said with a slight chuckle.

"And you still have such an amazing figure... Okay, now I can see why the blondes might hate you," I teased.

"You're so funny. You're pretty smoking hot yourself, but your sweater set isn't showing you off."

"Maybe you could come shopping with me sometime?"

"I would love that."

"Okay, it's a date. Um... I'm going to head inside. Will you be all right getting home?"

"Yeah, I'm only a few doors down. Thanks for... for being so nice, Bella. I appreciate it."

"Right back at you. Get home safe."

With a wave, Mia hightailed it down the street and I stood and watched her for a second.

This was one hell of an evening. Intrigue everywhere I turned. I didn't believe for a second Mia's sliders were the cause of Emily and Sarah's sudden stomach trouble. My instinct had a different culprit in mind, and I doubt it was an accident.

CHAPTER FIVE

WHEN HER FRONT DOOR SWUNG open the following afternoon, I was greeted by a very different Nicole.

"Hi, how are the girls feeling?" I asked, standing on her front porch with her basket.

"Still not great. It was a long night," Nicole replied in a weary tone.

"I wanted to return your basket and thank you for inviting me last night."

She reached for it and then exhaled. "Do you have a second? You want to come in?"

"Sure. That would be nice."

As Nicole took the basket from me, she said, "I could use another cup of coffee. How about you?"

"I'm good," I responded and followed her to the kitchen. "If I have coffee now, I'll be up all night."

"I was up all night. This is my fourth cup."

After she poured her coffee, we ventured into the back room and sat on the sofa. "So, are the girls sleeping?" I asked.

"Yeah, for now. It doesn't matter how old you are, when you're sick, you always want your mom. Dave wasn't a lot of help."

With the afternoon sun streaming through her window, the light hit her face, and on her left cheek, it was easy to see she was masking something beneath her makeup.

My gaze was fixed on it, and she must have sensed it because she moved to the nearby chair.

"You know I love this room," she said, "but in the afternoon, you practically need sunglasses. You're welcome to move over here if you want."

"I'm okay. You were getting the worst of it. Are you feeling okay? Did you catch a bug from Emily and Sarah?"

"I don't think so. My stomach is fine. It's just... Dave and I had a terrible fight in the middle of the girls' stomach issues. I guess I'm feeling low. I can't shake it."

"What did you fight about?"

"He blamed me for them getting sick. Actually, he blamed Mia. He said she brought poisoned sliders. I called Catherine this morning and got her to admit she's the one that invited that gold digger. I told her never again. Dave doesn't want her in this house."

"Um, I can't imagine the sliders were poisoned. Did anyone else eat them?"

"I'm not sure. I was kind of wondering what you thought. Catherine told me she saw you and Mia talking last night in the street when everyone left. What did she say?"

How should I answer this burning question? I didn't want to choose sides or alienate anyone. Being Switzerland in a group of women was like walking an oily tightrope.

"Um... nothing much. I apologized for not getting a chance to talk to her more. She seemed friendly, but a little guarded, if that makes sense."

"Yeah, I guess. Did she say anything about me?"

"Not that I can recall. I'll be honest, I'm not the best at reading people sometimes or navigating my way through social situations. I don't think I got a chance to talk to Julie that much either. I mostly talked to Wendy and Catherine."

"Was Wendy crying on your shoulder? She gets a little melancholy when she drinks."

"Um, not really," I replied and kept the truth to myself.

"She didn't bring up her husband, Lance?"

"Only in passing. She seems like a sweet woman."

"Wendy is as dumb as a stump. You see, Lance is a therapist and I found out Mia is one of his patients. If she wants to know who the other woman is, she doesn't need to look any further than the gold digger down the street."

While Nicole was having an off day, her comments about her "friends" were beyond. I loved good gossip as much as the next person, but I couldn't engage in this. It was wrong.

"So, are you and your husband, Dave, doing okay now? You know, post-fight. It usually takes me a couple of days to get over an upset."

She glanced down at the floor. "Yeah, I guess. Until the next time."

"He kind of startled me last night. I couldn't fit the ice into the freezer, so I guessed that you had one in the garage, and he found me in there. Dave's pretty intimidating."

"What's that supposed to mean?"

"Nothing. Just that he's a big guy with a booming voice. It caught me off guard. My dad was like that, and my mom was tiny like you. When they fought, sometimes things got out of hand."

I was lying my ass off about my dearly departed parents, but maybe this would open a door for Nicole to talk to someone. The longer I sat here, the more obvious it was that Dave had hit her last night and it probably wasn't the first time. Could this be why she was so quick to criticize everyone else?

Nicole cleared her throat and rose. "Um, that must have been very difficult for you growing up. Anyway, I'm going to start dinner. I want to see if the girls can handle some soup, so if you'll excuse me."

I got up from the couch. "Of course. I need to go since my husband is coming home from DC a night early, I want to get dinner started too."

As we left the room and landed back in the kitchen, one of Nicole's daughters called for her.

"Oh, that sounds like Sarah. Would you mind showing yourself out?"

"Not at all. And, Nicole, if you ever need to talk about anything. I'm right across the street. I'd never tell a soul."

She squeezed her eyes tight for a second and inhaled. "Thank you. I... uh... I have to go."

She rushed off to her daughter, leaving me alone. My eyes darted around the kitchen, wondering if there were any answers to my questions in this room? A clue? Something.

When I spied the pile of mail, it looked untouched from last night. My curiosity got the best of me, and I rifled through it.

Hmm... what do you know? Did I just find what I was looking for?

CHAPTER SIX

"HEY, BABY. I'M BACK," JACK whispered.

Tucked in bed, I was lulled awake by the sweet sound of my husband's voice. As soon as I got home from Nicole's, he texted to say he'd be late.

With my eyes fully opened and focused, I caressed his handsome face. "Hi. I'm sorry, I fell asleep."

"Don't be," he replied in a warm tone. "I'm sorry I'm so late."

"But you're here. That's what counts."

When Jack climbed into bed and held me in his arms, I took in his scent. He smelled like fresh laundry that was dried in the sunshine on a spring morning.

"Go back to sleep, sweetie. We have all weekend."

"You promise?"

"Of course. I'll be right here."

THE NEXT MORNING, HE BROUGHT me a coffee in bed.

"I could get used to this," I said when the chicory aroma hit my nose.

Jack chuckled. "You are used to it."

I took a sip. "Good point. Mmm… this is so good. It tastes like the coffee from Café Du Monde in New Orleans."

"It is. One of my old clients sent it to me," Jack replied as he joined me in bed.

"Nice. I love it. Remember our first trip to New Orleans? I think I ate my weight in beignets."

"The beignets aren't the only thing I remember. How about that big suite?"

Either the coffee or the memories flushed my cheeks. "We made the most of it. I will never forget the older couple we rode up on the elevator with, Artie and Audrey."

"Neither will I. Only you and I could spend an entire evening in pleasant conversation with a couple, and then discover they'd been in the room next to ours the entire weekend. You know they heard us."

"Oh, yeah. I remember when the dawn finally broke and I asked, 'Have you been next-door this entire weekend?' and Audrey goes, 'That's right. Enjoy your big room!' I nearly fainted."

"But we gave them a hell of an encore."

I giggled. "That we did, Mister Wright."

"So how was your week? Did you meet any of the neighbors?"

"Yup. I got a big old eye full of some things I wished I hadn't seen."

He grinned. "I'm intrigued. Like what?"

"Well, in general, The Heights seems like a very fancy neighborhood with extra fancy people, but underneath it, it's kind of sad. I went to Wine Down Wednesday across the street and I met some of the ladies that live close by. The gossip and the backstabbing are at one hundred. I've only met one of the husbands and got a bad vibe. I'm not sure if you'll find any golfing buddies in that group."

"I don't want any. When I'm here on the weekends, I want it to be just the two of us."

"What if there's a party or something on a Saturday night?"

"Honey, please. You know I need time to unwind. I don't want to get roped into small talk with a bunch of strangers. I want you all to myself."

"Okay. I'm sure I'll get my fill of the ladies on the weekdays."

"Did you connect with any of them?"

"I thought I did with Nicole, the lady who invited me to her house. Now I'm not so sure. One of the ladies, Catherine, made me laugh, but I wouldn't trust her with any deep, dark secrets. And Mia, who is kind of an outcast, seems nice."

"Maybe invite Mia over sometime."

"I'm planning on it. Oh, and the word about me being obsessed with true crime is out. One woman, Wendy, thinks her husband is cheating on her and asked me to investigate. Can you believe it?"

"That could be risky business. What if you're wrong?"

"You don't trust my sleuthing skills?"

"Of course I do. But a cheating husband in the neighborhood? I don't know, sweetie. It could all come crashing down on you. The husband could deny it and then your new friend, Wendy, might believe him. The next thing you know, you have no friends in The Heights."

"I didn't think of it like that. I did cut Deborah out of my life when she told me she suspected you and Melissa were having an affair. And then Deborah died such an awful, painful death. Remember she had a fatal fall in her house?"

"While I feel badly about Deborah, there was nothing going on between me and Melissa. You were right to believe me. Deborah, may she rest in peace, was trying to stir up trouble between us. I said to you at the time, she was a bored housewife and jealous of you."

Would there always be a teeny sliver of doubt about Jack's affair with Melissa? In my heart, I did believe him. In my head, I suppose I would always wonder.

Jack pushed himself off the bed. "I don't know why we're rehashing the past. This was over a decade ago. I hope you're not going to harp about this all weekend."

"I'm not harping about anything. Please, let's forget about it."

He slipped on his shorts and grabbed his tennis shoes from the closet. "I need some air. I'm going for a run."

"Jack, don't go. Come back to bed."

He ignored me and got ready for his workout in silence. God, I hated when he did this. Once he was angry, there was no talking to him.

"I'd like the house to be in order when I get back," he said in a low, cold tone. "I don't think it's too much to ask that the place not look like a pigsty."

"Of course, it isn't, but I don't want you to leave when you're this mad. Please."

I clung to my pillow while he stormed out, praying he would come back to me, but he didn't. I was alone... again.

CHAPTER SEVEN

THEY WERE THE BEST OF times, they were the worst of times.

What a perfect quote to sum up our fifteen years of marriage. When things were good, they were outstanding, and when they were bad, it was hell.

After a day of silence, Jack went back to DC. I had no idea when he would come home. Patience might be a virtue, but this sucked.

Why did I have to bring up Melissa? Our therapist said her name was a trigger for Jack, and once I said I believed him, and they didn't have an affair, it was in the past. In general, bringing up the past never served us well, unless we were reliving the glory days of New Orleans or other amazing moments together.

Deep down there would always be two doubts when it came to Jack. Did he have an affair with Melissa, and did he resent me for being unable to conceive a child? Infertility led me to a harrowing place. My mind played tricks on me, and I convinced myself Jack would end up having an affair and a baby with someone else. Even though he swore he was fine with it being just us.

When I was thirty-five and the doctors gave me the news that they didn't think it would ever happen for us, Melissa befriended me.

She was an acquaintance from my yoga studio and going through a divorce. At first, we commiserated and shared our heartaches. Later it seemed like she had a fondness for my husband and needed help around her house.

Deborah was the one claiming she had proof of their dirty deeds, but she fell to her death before she could show me. It was what Jack would call a clusterfuck of a situation.

Our relationship turned into a bumpy roller coaster before it smoothed out like a pleasant ride on the merry-go-round. Now we were back here again.

By Tuesday, I was knee-deep in discarded snack bags and dirty dishes. Jack was right about one thing, this place was a pigsty, and I was Mrs. Piggy.

Like a tornado, I stormed through the house making it and myself presentable. My timing was impeccable. A short half hour later, there was a knock at the door.

I was delighted to find Catherine on my porch.

"Hey, how are you, Catherine?"

"Not bad." She smiled.

"Would you like to come in?"

"Yeah, I'll take a quick load off before I head home to Mick."

As she waltzed into my grand foray, I gestured toward the living room couch. "Have a seat. Can I get you anything?"

"I could go for a stiff drink, but I think I'll wait until I get home and see if I can score a stiff Mick instead," she joked.

"I like the way you think," I replied as we got comfy on the sofa.

All done up in her professional, business attire, Catherine looked the spitting image of someone who knew how to work hard and play hard.

"What brings you by?" I asked.

"Well," she sighed. "I'm on the outs with the blonde trio. Nicole is mad at me for inviting Mia to Wine Down Wednesday last week, so I thought maybe you and Mia could come over to my place tomorrow night. I mean, unless you've already been invited to Nicole's then don't worry about it."

I shrugged. "Uh… I haven't. I haven't seen her since Thursday. I went over to see how her girls were doing. I get the feeling I won't be part of the inner circle anytime soon."

"Honey, you don't want to be in that circle. It's toxic. I was only going because I work with Dave and I'm the nosiest bitch on the block. I couldn't resist the gossip."

"What do you think of him?"

"Dave? He's okay. Why do you ask?"

"Um, no reason. Usually, salesmen are pretty friendly even if they're faking it. I didn't find him to be very hospitable."

"Well, who told you Dave was a salesman?"

"I thought Nicole said he was a real estate agent?"

She let out a laugh. "Dave? That man couldn't sell kibble to a starving dog. He's the office manager. That's what I meant by being in the trenches with him."

I furrowed my brow because I was the only housewife in The Heights that could. "Oh, I guess I misunderstood."

Did that explain the fat check I saw tucked into a card for Nicole from a Sylvie Stickle? How else could the Taylor family afford to live in this neighborhood?

"You must've misunderstood," Catherine replied. "I call him my bitch boy. But not to his face. I say it behind his back like a decent human being. I'm not a monster."

"I can't imagine anyone calling Dave a bitch boy to his face. He's a pretty big guy. Is he a good manager?"

"Why all the questions about Dave? Do you know something I don't?"

Even if I did, I'd never tell Catherine. She was a definite hoot, but I'd never trust her with a secret.

I cleared my throat. "Um… I was just curious."

"So, drinks tomorrow at my place?" she asked and rose from the couch.

"Sure, that sounds great. I'm not exactly sure where you live though."

"Where's your cell phone?"

"It's in the dining room. Let me grab it."

She followed me. "Sure. Oh, Bella. Your table setting is beautiful. I'd love to stick around long enough to meet your husband."

My cheeks flushed in embarrassment. I didn't have the heart to tell her I did the table scape on Sunday, hoping Jack would come back to me.

"Um… yeah. That would be great, but I set that up for my brother. He keeps promising he'll pop in to check out the new house. He lives in Gettysburg."

"Is he single? You should try to fix him up with Julie. Maybe if she got laid, she wouldn't be such a tight ass."

"Don't hold back. Tell me what you really think," I teased.

"All I'm saying is unless that girl is drunk, she barely says two words to me, and when she does it's all about her."

I plucked up my phone, tapped my contacts, and handed it to her. "I can hardly wait until tomorrow night. Put your info here. And I'll shoot you a text tomorrow."

Her fingers fired across the keyboard. "I'm not too far. You could probably walk. We live across the street from Mia." She handed me back the phone. "How does seven sound?"

"Perfect. I can't wait. I'll be sure to bring something to snack on."

"That sounds great. I've got plenty of wine. In fact, we should do a tasting. I just got some Australian whites that are out of this world."

As I walked Catherine out, my mind raced with an excuse for why I wouldn't be drinking tomorrow night.

With the women of The Heights, I thought it best to remain clearheaded and in control.

CHAPTER EIGHT

"SO… IT'S KIND OF EMBARRASSING, but I have a UTI and I'm on antibiotics. I won't be able to try your delicious wine," I fibbed to Catherine and Mia at Wine Down Wednesday.

"Oh, you poor thing," Catherine said. "Although, I was prone to them when I first got married, if you know what I mean. Cranberry juice and a little break from my Mick Dick fixed me right up."

Nervous laughter filled the air, and I clicked my tongue. "I guess I don't get enough time with Jack, but we make up for it on the weekends. Thanks for the cranberry juice tip. I appreciate it."

Catherine topped off Mia's wine and picked up her glass. "Let's go by the fire. It sure got cold today."

"I'll grab the desert tray," Mia offered. "Everything looks yummy."

Mia appeared more relaxed than last week, but sorrow illuminated from her beautiful, dark eyes.

Once we were settled and comfy, I commented, "Your house is breathtaking. I love the layout and how cozy it is."

"Thanks. It's not as over-the-top as Nicole's place. I wanted it to feel like a home if that makes sense."

"I totally get it," Mia replied. "Samuel's taste is a little too old-fashioned for me, but yours is impeccable. If I have a redo, I'll probably copy you."

"What's stopping you, hon?" Catherine asked.

She shrugged. "Well… I know what people say about me. If they saw a bunch of furniture deliveries or flooring company, I'd be more ostracized than I already am. I guess no one understands our relationship."

"Mia, it's none of their business," I assured her.

After a sip of wine, she exhaled. "I would like to talk about it."

Catherine leaned forward. "We're here for you."

Something told me Catherine was here for the juicy details.

Mia nodded and set her wine down. "Um… okay. It's been so long since I had anyone to talk to. Samuel and I met about five years ago when he lived on Clayton Avenue in the big house that looks like a museum or something. I was his home health care worker. He has two grown sons that live in Hope Ridge and neither one worked at the time. They all lived in the house together and didn't lift a finger to take care of Samuel. He battled colon cancer, and when I met him, he was recovering from a hip replacement. When I would arrive first thing in the morning, poor Samuel would be in agony. Those lazy, good-for-nothing sons couldn't even get him his pain medication."

"That's disgusting," I exclaimed. "How do people like that live with themselves?"

"They were unbothered or hungover," Mia replied. "I honestly felt like they were sitting around his house waiting for him to die."

Catherine shook her head. "Oh, hon. That's plain awful."

"You've got that right," Mia added. "I started going to see Samuel when I wasn't working to check on him. I was only scheduled for an hour a day, but I couldn't help but wonder what the rest of his hours were like. Martin, his eldest, seemed as suspicious of me as I was of him. He called the agency I worked for and requested someone else, but I kept checking in on him. I'd bring him books or puzzles to keep him occupied. We talked a lot, and I became very fond of him. And I know what you're thinking — he's fifty years older than me — but for a girl who grew up without her dad, Samuel meant a lot to me."

"I get that. But what about your social life?" I asked. "I mean, you couldn't have been more than twenty years old. Men must've been throwing themselves at you and probably still are."

Mia sipped her wine and paused. "I was married. I got married right after high school. Trent was the captain of the football team, and I was the head cheerleader. I know it sounds so cliche, but we were happy."

Catherine halted mid-drink. "What do mean were? Did you divorce?"

Tears welled up in Mia's eyes. "Trent was killed in a car accident."

I gasped. "Oh, no. That's tragic. I'm so sorry. He was so young. You must've been devastated."

Mia collected herself. "You have no idea. It was the worst thing that ever happened to me. The day I went to Samuel's house to tell him, I had to let myself in. The door was unlocked, and I found him in his bedroom on the floor writhing in pain. His sons were still passed out from the night before and he'd fallen. Once I helped him and told him about my husband, we made a pact to take care of each other. Samuel wasn't safe in his own home. He confessed what I suspected. He was being abused by his own sons, and my life had fallen apart in an instant. So, we got married six months later. Samuel let them have the house and we moved here."

"I hope you won't think I'm being insensitive," Catherine said, "but is it fair to expect you to give up your life when you're so young? I don't know how old either one of you are, but my God, Mia, you have your entire life ahead of you."

"I don't feel like I'm giving up anything," Mia responded. "I'm almost thirty-one and Samuel is eighty. Shortly after we got married, his cancer returned and it's in his liver, and unfortunately, he doesn't have much time."

I choked back tears. "Oh, Mia. I'm so sorry."

"I appreciate that. The thing is, I do love him, and I know he loves me too. We've protected and taken care of each other. Samuel's sons won't be left a dime. His will is airtight, but when he goes, I worry about what will happen to me. That's why I've been in therapy, among other things. I know I'm going to lose him, and to be honest I haven't fully grieved my first husband."

"Of course you haven't, hon," Catherine said. "I had no idea you were going through this. I owe you a huge apology. I thought—"

"You thought I was only in it for the money," Mia finished her sentence.

Catherine nodded in shame. "Yeah. I realize now that makes me an asshole for judging you. I'm a straight shooter and when I screw up, I'll say so. You deserve our support. I mean, you have my support. Anything you need, let me know."

"That goes for me too," I added.

She wiped away a tear. "You have no idea what that means to me. Thank you. Samuel is so private. He doesn't want anyone to know the truth about his sons, Martin and Mason. Besides you two, the only person who knows what's going on is Lance, my therapist. It feels good to talk to actual friends instead of someone I'm paying."

Catherine reached over and squeezed her hand. "We are your friends, right, Bella?"

"Absolutely," I replied. "I'm on my own a lot, so don't hesitate to come on over anytime."

Did we just have a genuine friend moment? My guard was up like a brick wall of concrete when it came to female friendships, but my heart broke for Mia. To lose one husband in a fatal car accident, and a second currently facing the end because of cancer. It didn't get much more heartbreaking.

The evening was more enlightening and pleasant than I imagined. The conversation flowed smoothly between the three of us. I couldn't remember the last time I enjoyed hanging out with someone besides Jack.

Our female bonding was cut short due to a thin man entering the room. "Knock, knock! It's just me, girls."

With his "Hamilton" the musical T-shirt, and coiffed, highlighted hair, this exuberant fellow looked as if he'd left the audience of a Broadway show.

Catherine hopped up from the couch to greet him. "Hey, there's my man. How was the gang at Duffy's?"

"Oh, you know, drunk and silly like always." He giggled.

Wait... was this Mick? My image of this ballsy dame's husband was so different.

I chastised myself for making a snap judgment. Watching the two of them interact while Catherine introduced us, it was clear they were mad for one another.

Hey, whatever floats your boat.

Realizing I hadn't slept much, I concealed a yawn before saying good night to our gracious host. Mia followed my lead and we left together.

I paused under the streetlight in front of my house. "You didn't need to walk all the way back to my place."

"That's okay. I could use a little extra fresh air. It's cold, but it's a nice night."

"It definitely is. Hey, I meant what I said earlier. If you ever need anything, please don't hesitate to reach out."

She smiled. "That means a lot to me. Thank you. My anxiety gets the best of me sometimes and then I go inward."

"I understand. Mine too. Like I said, my husband is out of town most of the time. So, I'm usually free Monday through Friday."

"Good to know. I'm going to relieve Samuel's night nurse. I can't believe it's only nine o'clock. It feels like midnight."

"Yeah. I'm glad Catherine invited us over," I replied and glanced at Nicole's house. "Hmm... I wonder if Nicole had her Wine Down Wednesday. It looks kind of dark over there."

"You're right. I can't imagine I'd go again. Would you?"

"Oh, I don't know. Wendy seemed nice. Never say never."

"Suit yourself. Night."

As Mia journeyed home, I stole another peek at Nicole's place wondering if the blonde trio were inside gossiping about us. If they ever said anything about Mia in my presence, I would defend her. They had her all wrong.

When I turned to head inside, I stopped short and saw a light flickering at Nicole's house. After peering closer, I swore I saw someone at the window. Was Nicole watching me?

I shook the notion off and headed inside.

"Relax, Bella," I mumbled to myself. "No one is watching you. You're just a boring housewife."

That was exactly what I wanted them all to think.

CHAPTER NINE

AFTER I WAS IN MY comfy sweatpants and favorite hoodie, a knock on the door startled me.

"Bella, it's me, Nicole," she said from the porch. "Are you there?"

I opened the door a crack. "Nicole… um… are you all right?"

"Yeah, I'm sorry to bother you so late. I have a favor to ask. Could I come in?"

Am I curious or annoyed?

"Uh… sure. Come on in," I said.

I was too nosy for my own good. I had to find out what she wanted.

"Thank you, so much," she replied and came inside. "I promise I won't take up too much of your time."

"Have a seat on the couch. Can I get you anything? Some tea?"

Nicole made herself at home. "I'd love some wine if you have any."

"Oh… um… I'm so sorry. I don't have any wine. I'm not much of a drinker."

A nervous cackle escaped. "It's like you're speaking another language. No worries, then, I'm fine. I don't need anything."

I joined her on the couch. "Then, what can I help you with?"

"It's Emily. All of a sudden, she's been more cheerful, and I know this sounds terrible, but it's not like her."

Emily, the Eeyore sour puss. Her mother had a point.

"Are you worried she's on drugs or something?" I asked.

"Well, I was, but then I finally got it out of her. She has some sort of boyfriend. She met him on Instagram. And I realize what I'm about to say makes me a terrible mom. She showed me his picture and he's so good-looking, like movie star handsome. And I can't help but wonder, why Emily? The poor girl takes after her father. Look I love her and think she's beautiful, but… Please tell me I'm not the worst parent in the world."

"You're not. And you're right to be concerned about her activities online. There are a ton of creeps out there."

She sighed. "Thank you for saying that. It's like this dude seems almost too good to be true. He's filling her head with all these ideas about running away together."

"How do you know that? Did she share the messages?"

"Uh… I know their passwords. Every once in a while I log in and check their social. It's part of our deal. We pay for the phone, so we need to have access. They think I haven't invaded their privacy for years, but I still do it."

"That's smart. Not everyone is who they say they are. Social media is the wild west. Better to be safe than sorry."

"Right. Dave thinks I'm always overreacting, but this time is different. It's tough, I don't want the girls to know I still look, and most of the time there's nothing to be alarmed about, but this Colin Smith is a different story. He could be anyone. Wendy told me you're into true crime and stuff like that. I was hoping you might have some advice."

"Uh… I'm not on social media, but I could do a reverse Google image search on one of his photos. I learned that from the show, *Catfish*. It's pretty simple."

She whipped out her phone. "Here's his profile."

I took her cell and scrolled through his photos. "Well, I'm not an expert, but I'm pretty sure this is a model, and someone pilfered his photos. Look, he only has a hundred posts, and posts a couple of times a day."

"What does that mean?"

"It means this account is fairly new. Someone just created it." I handed her the phone. "Email me one of the photos. It's Bella 42 at Gmail dot com."

Her fingers flew across the keyboard. "Okay. I think if I tap the three dots in the upper right corner... yup... and... send."

When I opened up my laptop, I was careful to angle it away from her so she couldn't see my desktop. "All right, hang on. Got it. I'll save it and go to Google. So, let's see if Colin Smith is who he says he is. This will only take a second."

Professional photos loaded, with a bio and more information.

"I'm sorry," I said and showed Nicole. "Colin Smith is really Dax Wentworth, a model in Australia."

Her shoulders hunched and she inhaled. "Damn it. I was afraid of that. Then I'm guessing Colin isn't a personal trainer from Florida."

"No. Colin could be anybody. His real name could be Bart and he might live in his mother's basement."

"I don't know what to do."

"Look, Nicole, I'm not a mom, but if it was me, I'd be honest with Emily. Or blame me if you want to. Say it came up in conversation, and I was like a dog with a bone because I'm into true crime."

"Really? You wouldn't mind if I threw you under the bus like that?"

"Of course not. Keeping Emily safe is priority number one."

"Thank you. I don't know what to say. I totally owe you one."

"Deal... um... how soon could I collect on that favor?"

Nicole chuckled and made a strange face. "Geez, I don't know. I'm guessing you want me to say now?"

I shrugged. "I mean, kind of... it's about Mia."

She rolled her eyes. "That gold digger. I appreciate you, Bella. I truly do, but I don't want to be around her anymore. My husband, Dave, said I have to make nice with Catherine, but Mia? I don't know."

"All I'm asking is to give her a chance. Catherine had us over for Wine Down Wednesday, and her story is not as cut and dried as you think. Did you know when she was working for Samuel her first husband was killed in a car accident?"

The second I said the words car accident, she sucked in a breath and went pale. "Oh, God. I had no idea. That's heartbreaking."

"Yeah. She also told us Samuel's adult sons were abusing him. Mia and Samuel vowed to take care of each other. I don't think her husband is going to live much longer. I thought it would be good if she had support from the neighborhood when he passes."

"Yes, I suppose you're right. I'll talk to Wendy and Julie. Is it okay to tell them what you told me?"

"Uh... Mia didn't say it was a secret, so I guess it's okay. It's not like we're spreading gossip. This is straight from the horse's mouth. I think Mia could use a few friends."

As she gave me a slight nod, I could almost see her wheels turning. "Yeah. It sounds like it. I guess I misjudged her. You must think I'm an awful person."

"Not at all. You were my first friend in the neighborhood. That means something to me. And if you ever need anything, I'm here for you."

She rose and clicked her tongue. "What could I possibly need? I assure you, I'm fine."

Translation — my husband didn't hit me last week. Was that what she wanted me to believe?

I hauled myself off the couch. "You do seem to have it all figured out. Great house, kids, husband. You've got the whole package."

"Yes... well... it's getting late. Thank you again for helping me with Emily. I'd like to apologize in advance for the stink eye she's going to throw your way the next time you come over."

I followed Nicole as she headed for the door. "Hey, no worries. Sometimes people shoot the messenger. Can you imagine if I was a real detective uncovering everyone's secrets?" I laughed.

"You'd probably be getting it from all sides. Again, thank you. I'll make sure Emily blocks Colin Smith and reports his fake account to Instagram."

I opened my front door for her. "That sounds like a great idea."

She stepped out onto the porch. "It's so weird to think Colin Smith could've been anybody. Well, good night."

"Night," I said as I watched her head home.

Nicole was right. Colin Smith could've been anyone, literally anyone in the world.

CHAPTER TEN

"ON OCTOBER FOURTEENTH, 2021, Lily Miller went missing after attending her homecoming dance in Raleigh, North Carolina."

Coming home from a power walk on Friday afternoon, I was in my zone listening to one of my favorite podcasts, "Chime in on Crime," with True Maverick. The buttery tones of her voice put me into a trance. It was as if I was there in the flesh, living every moment.

"Because of her quick-thinking parents, they downloaded the ping app and put in Lily's cell number to track her location. Unfortunately, they came up empty, which suggested foul play to the authorities."

When I got back to my house, I pulled out my earbuds and turned off the podcast. From this angle, I saw the shutters were open, and I distinctly remember leaving them closed.

Was someone in my house? What would True Maverick do?

My hands trembled as I pulled up the keypad on my phone and dialed 911. If someone was in there, all I had to do was hit send. With my free hand on the doorknob, I opened the door I knew I locked.

"Hello… anyone here?" I hollered. "I'm about to call the police."

"Babe! Is that you?"

"Yes!"

Thank God! Jack was home!

In a casual way, he sauntered down the steps, handsome as ever. "Hi, honey. I missed you," he said as if we didn't have a big fight.

"Hey, I missed you too."

"Where were you?"

"I went out for a walk. Um… I can't believe you're here right now. I wasn't sure if…"

"Hush," he said, and pulled me into his arms, shutting our front door. "I'm sorry. And that's all I want to say about it. Work has been insane and I'm here, so let's enjoy each other."

"That's all I ever wanted. You and me, just us."

"We have the entire weekend."

I broke our embrace. "I wasn't sure if you were coming, so I mean… I didn't grocery shop or shave my legs or even shower yet."

"Why don't you get cleaned up, and I'll worry about everything else."

I raised an eyebrow. "Just what do you have planned, Mister Wright?"

"You'll see, Mrs. Wright."

WHILE I WAS SOAKING IN the tub, I debated if I should say anything about last weekend. He didn't even call or text me after he headed back to DC. It was a total ice out, and I hated every second. When he withheld his affection, it took me to a bad place.

As I weighed my options, he crept into the bathroom with a tray of goodies. Wearing nothing but his boxers, I decided to enjoy my weekend with him and forget about the fight. Nothing good could come from it, but plenty of good could come from him joining me in the tub.

"So, whatcha got there, Sir," I said in a flirty tone.

"A special treat for my girl," he replied with an irresistible grin emerging on his face.

"Are you talking about what's on the tray or in your boxers?"

"Maybe a little of each." He chuckled, got naked, and plucked up a juicy strawberry from the tray.

Standing at the edge of the tub, he offered it to me. "Take a bite. I want to see you take it all."

As I licked my lips and opened my mouth for him, he slowly teased my mouth with the strawberry. When we played like this, I knew what he craved. Sometimes my husband took me with tender passion and sometimes we fucked, hard.

After I swallowed the delicious fruit and sucked on his fingers, I saw his cock swell into a full erection.

"You want to fuck me, don't you?" I asked, my voice laced with desire.

"I don't want to, I have to. Turn around and hang onto the edge. Please remember how much I love you."

When I did as he asked, Jack let some of the water out of the tub, so he could have full access. Once it was at a satisfactory level, he slid his hand down the length of my spine and cupped my ass.

Jack might've thought this was about what he needed, but I did too. He took me with gentle thrusts before gripping my hips and pounding away until we both came undone.

Welcome home, Mister Wright!

CHAPTER ELEVEN

MONDAY AFTERNOON I WAS STILL floating on a cloud of Jack bliss. Chef's kiss to the weekend! It was everything I hoped for and more.

Jack headed back to DC with a smile on his face and my scent on his lips. It wouldn't surprise me if he came home on Wednesday. He did say Thursday at the latest.

While my marriage was the picture of perfection, I wondered about my new friends as I power-walked through The Heights. So far, we had a possible abusive husband, a cheating husband, and one that seemed like he missed his calling on stage. As I'd learned by following my true crime blogs and podcasts, without more evidence, I couldn't be sure about any of the husbands, except for Mia's.

As I passed by her place on my way home, I thought about her husband, Samuel, and his health. Poor Mia had been through so much.

Should I pop in and see if she needed anything? Before I could decide, I saw a car pulling into my driveway, so I picked up my pace and headed home. It looked just like Jack's car. Was he here to surprise me? He'd just left this morning.

When I got closer, I realized it was my brother, Anthony. I chuckled to myself because sometimes he did like to copy my husband when it came to anything with wheels. I was so relieved the motorcycle days were behind us.

I called to him, "Hey, big brother!"

He waved from the porch. "Hi."

It was his first visit to the new house. I couldn't wait to show him everything.

"I was hoping you'd pop in," I said.

"I'm sorry I took so long. Work has been crazy," he replied with an apologetic smile.

"Now where have I heard that before?" I joked and grabbed the key from under one of my potted plants.

"You keep your key out here?" Anthony asked with a parental tone to his voice.

I opened the front door. "Relax. This is probably the safest neighborhood in the country. Nobody even has Ring doorbells or security cameras. Come on in."

When he crossed the threshold, he appeared pleased. "Nice. This is great. Do you love it?"

"Yeah. Are you hungry?"

"I could eat," he replied. "I skipped lunch today."

"Right this way." I led him down the hall to the kitchen, bypassing the front room where I kept my laptop and all my notebooks about the true crime cases I followed. Anthony found my hobby quite silly.

When we landed in my large kitchen, a sparkle touched his chestnut eyes. "This really makes the house. What smells so good?"

"Oh… I have some soup in the crockpot. Your timing is spot on. It should be ready soon."

While I grabbed my ladle and stirred, Anthony meandered around, taking in the space, and checked out the formal dining room. "Hey… uh… why is your table set for two?"

"I thought you were coming last week, remember?"

He sighed. "Right. Okay. And you're sure you're doing all right… you know, with everything?"

After our parents passed away, Anthony became extra protective of me. I went through a terrible depression. We expected Mom to leave us, due to cancer, but when Dad died first of a massive stroke, it was grief on top of grief. Therapy helped, but they could never find the right antidepressant or proper dosage for me.

With our sudden move, Anthony wasn't on board, but when he realized Hope Ridge wasn't that far from Gettysburg, he changed his tune.

"Anthony, trust me, I'm fine. You don't need to worry about me. Do you… do you still talk to Jack?"

He grinned. "Yeah, I do. And… I'm glad you're okay. We don't need to eat in the fancy dining room. The china is so nice, I'm worried I'll break it."

I grabbed my soup bowls from the cupboard. "Then have a seat. Dinner is served."

"You know it's only four-thirty. We're officially old," he teased.

"Speak for yourself. I skipped lunch too," I replied and set down his soup. "Just like Mom used to make."

"Does that mean there's sourdough too?"

"Yup. And it's fresh. Let me get it."

Once we were settled at the island, he took a heaping spoon full. "This is excellent. You did good, sis."

"Thanks," I responded and dipped my bread in the soup.

"Seriously, I'm proud of you. I know this move was challenging."

"Thanks. I know you weren't keen on it at first, but I like it here. The change of scenery has been good for me. I'm curious about this house, though, since it was such a good price. I mentioned it to one of my neighbors and she acted like she knew a secret."

"Huh… that's weird. I know a woman from The Heights. Her name is Leigh. She has her own law firm in Hope Ridge. I'm supposed to see her next week. Do you want me to ask her?"

"Yeah. Why do you need a lawyer?"

"Uh… I don't. It's kind of a date type thing."

"Anthony, you buried the lead. That's wonderful. It's about time you got out there. Brenda treated you like crap. You deserve to be happy."

"We all do, but do me a favor… please don't bring up my ex again."

"Sorry. I promise. I won't."

When Anthony and Brenda divorced, I did a dance of joy. She was a whole mess. The woman had a permanent resting bitch face with a personality to match. I never understood what my brother saw in her.

"How about my one and only favorite nephew, Danny? How's he doing?"

Anthony beamed. "He's loving the college life and is crazy about booze and broads, just like his old man."

I chuckled and changed the subject. "So… this… Leigh… how far does she live from me? Is she down the block or on the other side of the development?"

"The other side. I hope you don't mind, but I gave her your address and asked her to look in on you."

I rolled my eyes. "I appreciate your concern, big brother, but I don't need a babysitter. I'm starting to make friends."

"That's good because Leigh is too busy, I don't think she'll have time. She canceled our date twice. The woman is married to her job."

"What do you think about that?"

"I think it's great since I am too, and I don't live in Hope Ridge. I'm not looking for anything serious."

"Okay. But if she cancels again, you might want to punt this busy chick and start over."

"Now who's being too protective?" He chuckled. "So, tell me about these new friends. Any of them single, in case I don't go out with Leigh?"

"Well, one is. Her name is Julie. I haven't talked to her very much. Just know, the houses on the outside are gorgeous and perfect, and the lives of the people that live there are complicated. I mean, whose life isn't?"

"Good point."

When we finished our soup and catch-up session, I walked my brother out and waved one last time from the porch before he pulled out of my driveway. Relieved it went well, I exhaled, taking in this beautiful night, until I noticed Dave pulling up across the street.

After he parked and got out of his car, he stood motionless and stared. This man was a husband to Nicole, a father to Emily and Sarah, and a soon-to-be enemy of mine. I felt it in my bones.

CHAPTER TWELVE

IN OUR POSTCOITAL CUDDLE, I sighed. "I don't think I can move, Mister Wright. You've rendered me motionless."

Jack squeezed me a little tighter. "Good. Let's spend the rest of the weekend right here."

"What will we do for food?"

"I think there are some snacks in one of my overnight bags."

"Okay. Which one of us will have to get up?"

Before Jack responded, someone was ringing our doorbell in rapid succession.

I jolted upright and hopped out of the bed. "Who the hell is that? I better go see."

"You weren't expecting anyone, right?"

I slipped on my robe. "Of course not. I didn't even go to Wine Down Wednesday this week, so I don't think it's anyone from the neighborhood. Maybe it's a kid selling something for school?"

"Tell whoever it is to piss off," Jack said in a joking tone, but I knew he wasn't kidding.

"I'll be right back," I replied and rushed out of the room and down the stairs.

When I flung the door open, I was shocked to find Catherine on my porch with tears in her eyes. "Are you okay? What's going on?"

"It's Mia's husband, Samuel. He passed."

"Oh, no. I'm so sorry to hear that. How's Mia doing?"

"Not very well, I'm afraid. The hospice nurse was there and was a godsend, but Mia is falling apart. I told her I'd try to rally the troops. I know it's Saturday, and your husband is home, but could you come over? I don't think she should be alone."

I coughed and cinched the belt on my robe. "Um… you know, I don't think I'd be much help. Whatever I had on Wednesday is still lingering. I'd hate to get everyone sick."

"Is that why you have bedhead and aren't dressed at four o'clock in the afternoon?"

"Yes. That's exactly why. I feel worse today than I did on Wednesday. Jack didn't even come this weekend," I fibbed. "He's… uh… He was worried I'd get him sick."

"Your cheeks are flushed," Catherine said and took a step back. "Maybe it is best you get some rest."

"Yeah, I think so too. I'll touch base with you as soon as I feel better. Please tell Mia how sorry I am. And when you get news about the service, let me know, I'd like to send flowers."

"Sure. I was going to offer to have the luncheon after the funeral at my place. Maybe everyone in the neighborhood could bring something."

"Of course. Just tell me what you want me to bring."

"Okay. I'll text you tomorrow and see how you're feeling. Take care, Bella."

"You, too. See you soon."

As soon as she headed down the steps, I shut the door. For a moment, I paused before going back to Jack upstairs. My heart broke for Mia, but what could I do right now?

The weeks that followed my parents' funerals were when I needed people to check in on me. So much happens all at once after someone dies and then — nothing. I wouldn't let Mia be alone in her grief.

When I landed back in the bedroom, Jack asked, "Who was that?"

"It was Catherine, one of our neighbors. She wanted to tell me that Mia's husband passed away."

He sat up in bed. "Oh, no. I'm sorry. Which one is Mia?"

"She's the young one that was a caretaker to an older man and married him after her first husband died in a... anyway... Catherine wanted to rally the troops for Mia, but I told her I was sick."

"Couldn't you tell her the truth?"

"Well, saying I was sick seemed like a better excuse than wanting to shag my husband all weekend."

"You think they'd be jealous?"

I sauntered to the bed. "I know they would. The husbands in this neighborhood don't hold a candle to you. It's like an Algonquin Round Table of mismatched misfits."

Jack clasped my hand and tugged me to him. "You're just saying that so I'll make you come again."

His words made my skin break out in goosebumps. "Does that mean you're going to?"

"Absolutely. Let's get this robe off. I want to see my baby naked and kiss every inch of her."

I did as he asked. "I'm all yours."

Was guilt creeping in for basking in pleasure? Maybe. Was it worth it? A hundred percent.

CHAPTER THIRTEEN

"BELLA. THANK YOU FOR COMING," Catherine said Tuesday afternoon.

I handed her the pineapple upside-down cake she requested. "Of course."

To my dismay, Catherine put our Wine Down Wednesday clan into a group chat. My OCD went a little loony, especially when Julie veered off-topic. When communicating via text, I liked to keep it simple.

"How's Mia doing?" I asked as I followed her to the buffet table. "I'm sorry I couldn't make it to the service."

Catherine set my cake down and pulled me aside. "Honestly, she was doing pretty well until Samuel's sons showed up at the funeral home. She's going to need us."

"You can count on me. I've cleared my schedule for the rest of the week and next week too."

"That's so kind of you," Catherine replied. "Oh, Mitch is waving me over. I better see what he needs. Make yourself at home."

"Pineapple upside-down cake, my favorite," a tall, attractive, blonde man said and slithered a little too close to me. "Is it homemade?"

I took a step back. "Um… yeah… my mother's recipe."

He offered me his hand. "You must be Bella."

I shook it, noticing his hands were rather large and his skin was silky smooth. "Yes… and you are?"

"Lance Anderson, well… Doctor Anderson. You know my wife, Wendy."

The way his intense, sky-blue eyes captured mine made me uneasy. It was as if he knew what I looked like naked. With a gentle tug, he drew me to him, and I released his hand.

"It's nice to meet you, Doctor."

"Please, call me Lance. It's a pleasure to meet you as well. A real pleasure. I can't wait to try a piece of your cake."

Pure mischief danced on his lips before he sauntered away. What the hell was that?

After I brushed off the odd exchange, I surveyed the room of mourners, and it surprised me to see a mostly geriatric crowd. Maybe Mia didn't have many relatives. Were we her only friends?

As I made my way through the sea of canes and walkers looking for Mia, Julie intercepted me. "Hi, Bella. How are you? Did I see you chatting with Lance?"

"Hey, Julie. Only for a second. How have you been?"

"Okay, I guess. We missed you Wednesday. Are you feeling better?"

Julie missed me? When I looked back on our limited interaction at the first Wine Down Wednesday, it dawned on me, she was the most stuck-up of the blonde trio. Not talking to her that night wasn't my fault, it was hers. Was I supposed to believe we were suddenly best friends?

"I am. Thank you for asking. So… uh… did you go to the service?"

"No. To be honest, I never met Mia's husband and I don't know Mia very well either. It's still sad though. I wonder if Mia will stay in the neighborhood or move. I've been hearing some things."

"Like what?"

"Well… you know, she married him for the money. She's so young and will have a small fortune now. I can't imagine she'll stay in Hope Ridge forever. I wouldn't. I'd travel and take on a lover in every city."

"Why don't you?"

"What do you mean?" Julie asked with a puzzled expression.

"All I'm saying is I've heard some things too. You divorced someone rich, so why don't you travel and take on a lover in every city? What's keeping you in Hope Ridge?"

"I... I have roots here. I didn't just move to The Heights yesterday. I have friends... and... stuff going on," she huffed. "Exactly what are you insinuating?"

"Oh, gosh, nothing. Forgive me. I get uncomfortable at social gatherings. My anxiety is at a ten. I don't know why I said that."

Her eyes narrowed. "Yeah... okay... I get uncomfortable too. I'm going to see if Catherine needs any help in the kitchen. Excuse me."

One blonde down and two to go!

I wondered which ray of sunshine I'd run into next. The only person I cared to speak to was Mia. Where was she?

I headed towards the back of the house, and I found her sitting in a chair. An impromptu receiving line had formed, so I hopped in it and waited my turn to express my condolences.

When I glanced out the window, I noticed a group of men gathered on the patio. They looked around Jack's age and were drinking beer. Who would do that? Then, it hit me, they might be Samuel's grown sons and their friends.

With discretion, I observed their every move and even managed a couple of sneaky pics. My intuition told me the two unshaved guys with the wrinkled khakis were Samuel's entitled offspring. They had an old-money, lazy way about them.

I became so engrossed in my Google searches of Martin and Mason, I didn't notice I was at the front of Mia's line.

"Bella... hi... um... thanks for coming."

"Oh, gosh," I heaved and put away my phone. "I'm so sorry. I was distracted. How are you doing?"

"Well, you know. As well as can be expected. Samuel went peacefully. I'm grateful for that. It's the strangest thing. I'd been telling everyone the day before he died, his color was good, and he ate well. He even wanted to play cards. Then the next morning he went downhill fast."

"Oh, Mia, I don't know what to say."

"It's okay. I'm just glad you're here. I don't know that many people. I'm not close with my family and they all moved away years ago, so I appreciate you."

Since there was no one behind me, I crouched down and whispered, "Are Samuel's sons out on the patio?"

"Yeah. They brought their drinking buddies and a cooler. I'm disgusted. They didn't even shave or iron their pants. It would've broken Samuel's heart."

"That's so disrespectful. What if… what if you can't get them to leave?"

"Don't worry, I thought of that. Nicole's husband, Dave, said he'd stick around until they were gone."

"Oh, good. He's a big guy."

"My therapist, Lance, Wendy's husband, is here too. He's not quite as big as Dave, but he said he'd stay too. I'm worried about what Mason and Martin will do now. There's a reading of the will on Thursday."

"They don't know your husband cut them out?"

"I don't think so. We're meeting at the lawyer's office at three in the afternoon. I thought it seemed quick, but Martin and Mason insisted. It could turn ugly."

"Who is the lawyer?"

"Steven Katz. Do you know him? He has a small firm on Main Street."

"No, I don't. Let me know if you want someone to go with you. I'm free. I'll do it."

"Okay. I'll shoot you a text."

A fresh wave of mourners were lined up behind me. "I'll let you go. Just know I'm here for you."

"Thanks, Bella."

As I headed out, I spied Wendy, Nicole, Dave, and Lance in the formal living area. Luckily, they didn't see me. Dave might make a great bouncer, but he gave me the creeps.

Once I was on the porch, I exhaled. With my emotions bubbling to the surface, I wasted no time heading for home. I was about to cross the street when someone called my name.

"Bella! Hey, Bella, wait!"

I turned to find Nicole coming toward me, so I stopped. "Hi. I meant to come find you, but I don't know, seeing Mia reminded me of... of my parents' funerals."

"I didn't know you lost them. I guess I should consider myself lucky. My mom drives me crazy, but she's still with us."

"Yeah. You're very fortunate."

Did she just roll her eyes?

"So, Bella, the reason I wanted to talk to you. Well, I heard there was a handsome guy visiting you last week? I couldn't help but notice his car parked in your driveway. Was that your husband?"

"My husband? Uh... Oh! I think you're talking about my brother, Anthony."

Her face lit up with a wide grin. "Oh, your brother. I have to ask, is he single? Poor Julie hasn't dated anyone since her divorce, so I thought I'd play matchmaker for her."

I carefully considered her question. Did I want to subject my brother to this? While Julie was pretty in her own plastic way, I couldn't see them having a true connection. It was best to keep my worlds separate.

I cleared my throat. "You know, Anthony mentioned he was dating someone new. I'd hate to get in the middle of his love life. He hasn't been divorced that long. I don't think he's ready for anything serious."

"That's a shame. From across the street, he seemed like Julie's type."

What in the Gladys Kravitz is wrong with this woman!

"I'll be sure to let Anthony know he has an admirer. So, are we on tomorrow night for Wine Down Wednesday?"

"Oh... not this week. With the service and all, we decided to skip it. But Saturday night we're double dating with Wendy and her husband, Lance. Would you and your husband care to join us?"

Remembering what Jack said to me about keeping me to himself, I politely declined and said my good-byes.

Much like the day of my mom's funeral, it was clear and crisp. I took my time walking home enjoying the beauty of fall.

When I was in front of my house, the roar of an engine startled me. I whipped around to find an old truck speeding down the street.

With my phone at the ready, the truck screeched to a halt and one of the men from Mia's patio chucked a beer can out the window and yelled, "Hell, yeah. I can do whatever I want now. I'm rich."

As the truck raced away, I snapped a quick picture of its license plate with my cell.

I couldn't let Mia go alone to the reading of the will. Samuel's sons would eat her alive. Not on my watch!

CHAPTER FOURTEEN

"THANK YOU ALL FOR COMING," the lawyer, Steven Katz said in his office. "Today we gather to hear the last will and testament of the dearly departed, Samuel J. Wallace."

Daggers were coming out of Martin and Mason's eyes as we sat in the wingback chairs. Mia was visibly shaken by their presence, but they didn't scare me.

Rich, entitled white men were the biggest wusses on the planet, unless they were on something. Their beady eyes were bloodshot, but the pupils weren't dilated or constricted. If anything, they were probably hungover.

Steven continued, "I appreciate you all coming today. I will be brief. Mister Wallace was very clear and concise with his wishes."

"Okay, okay," one of the sons huffed. "Just get on with it. Mason and I have things to do."

Steven cleared his throat. "As you wish. To my darling wife, Mia, I pray you can make a fresh start. Thank you for your devotion to me. I love you."

"Oh, for Christ's sake," Mason griped. "Just get to the part about us."

Steven glanced at Mia, and she gestured for him to continue. "I'm afraid there's not much about you in here, Martin and Mason. It only says you're to vacate the house on Clayton Avenue by the end of the month. It's to be sold at auction and Mia can choose a charity to donate the funds to."

Martin jolted out of his seat. "That's not possible. You're lying."

"You can look at the document yourself if you like. There's one paragraph your father wrote about you and your brother, but I don't think you'll want to hear it."

"What's it say?" Mason asked. "Come on, Martin, sit down. Maybe it's something about our inheritance."

Martin plopped back into his chair, "Go ahead, Katz. Spill it."

Steven adjusted his glasses. "To my sons, Martin and Mason, I owe you an apology."

Mason nodded. "Damn right he does. Ever since he married that gold digger, our lives have been hell."

"Will you please be quiet," I snapped.

Martin glared at me. "Who the hell are you? Why are you even here?"

"I'm here at Mia's request, so shut it."

Sometimes I had trouble standing up for myself, but when it came to someone I cared about, I was a Mama bear.

When they both clammed up, I chuckled on the inside. Just as I thought, two wusses.

Steven sighed. "As I was saying, he wrote he owed you an apology. He goes on to say, from an early age I allowed your mother to spoil you, to receive rewards that were unearned. After her death, I realized we'd done both of you a disservice. So now I bequeath to you the value of a solid day's work. It's not too late for both of you to make an honest living and do better. I'm sorry I couldn't teach you that lesson while I was alive."

"What the hell is that supposed to mean?" Martin scoffed. "What about his millions?"

Steven removed his glasses. "He's left it all to Mia. I'm sorry, boys. He didn't leave you a dime."

"This is outrageous!" Mason said with venom in his voice. "Mia, if you think you're going to get away with this, guess again. Get ready for a fight."

I could barely conceal my grin. "How are you two planning on doing that? Daddy's not here to pay for your lawyer."

"Shut the fuck up," Martin jeered. "We can fight this, right, Steven?"

"I'm sorry, boys. Samuel made this new will right after he married Mia. He was of sound mind. It's airtight. Of course, anyone can sue anybody for anything, but it would be a waste of time. You'd only end up with a ton of legal bills."

"What about you?" Martin replied. "You've known us our entire lives. Can't you help us fight this, Steven?"

Steven remained steadfast. "My loyalties lie with your father and now with Mia. This is what he wanted. I can't help you."

"This is bullshit," Mason exclaimed. "Come on, Martin, let's go."

They both got up to leave, and Martin threw one last comment over his shoulder. "Don't get too comfortable, Mia. This isn't over."

When they exited and slammed the door, Mia exhaled. "Good, God. What do you think they'll do?"

"From a legal standpoint, nothing," Steven assured her. "From a reckless standpoint… well… you need to protect yourself."

"What do you suggest?" she asked.

"A security system, a dog, maybe think about getting a gun," he replied.

I clicked my tongue. "Do you really think those two lunkheads are dangerous?"

"I've known those two since they were born. They're not only dangerous, they're desperate."

CHAPTER FIFTEEN

"THANK YOU FOR SPENDING THE night here," Mia said. "After what happened in Steven's office today, I didn't want to be alone."

Tucked in bed, in Mia's quaint guest room, I insisted on staying with her after what Martin and Mason put her through. "It's my pleasure. I hope you don't mind, but I texted Catherine about the situation."

"No. Not at all. I'm going to see my therapist tomorrow and get his advice on what to do next. Even though I've lived in Hope Ridge my entire life, I'm thinking about moving."

"Where would you go?"

"I've always wanted to live on the west coast. Maybe somewhere in California. My best friend from grade school lives in San Francisco. We still keep in touch. I always said one of these days I would head west."

"Then you should do it. You have the world at your fingertips."

"Yeah. You know, the last few years feel like a blur. From the second my first husband died until I lost Samuel, it kind of seems like a bad dream."

"I get that. I think at one time or another everyone has moments like that."

"But you don't. I mean, you seem so together and you're like the happiest person I've ever met."

Boy, did I have her fooled. Maybe in some ways, we all hid behind masks. Of course, I loved my husband, but no marriage was easy. The move here was full of more ups and downs than an elevator.

"Oh, Mia, if you stick around the neighborhood a little longer, you'll see I have my moments too."

"So, I'm not alone?" she asked with her beautiful doe eyes widening.

"No. Definitely not alone. Do you think you'll be able to sleep?"

She shrugged. "I'm not sure. I have some of those over-the-counter sleep aids with melatonin, but I haven't tried one since Samuel became terminal. I wanted to be alert at all times."

"Maybe take a half. It'll take the edge off. You could probably use some sleep."

"Yeah. You're right about that. Do you need anything? There are fresh towels in your bathroom, and water in the mini-fridge."

"Hotel Mia is pretty sweet. I think I'm all set."

She chuckled. "Okay, night."

After she left, I popped in my earbuds and fired up "Chime in on Crime." My eyelids grew heavy after listening to True Maverick's velvety voice. She lulled me right to sleep.

WHEN THE SUN STREAMED THROUGH the shutters in Mia's guest room, I realized I'd slept through the night. That almost never happened. I pulled out my earbuds and sat up, wondering if Mia was awake.

I hauled myself out of bed and made my way downstairs to the kitchen. The second I saw the sliding glass door half opened, my breath hitched.

"Mia," I called and rushed up to the primary bedroom. "Mia!"

She wasn't there.

In a panic, I checked all the rooms and came up empty. With my heart racing, I called her cell, and it went right to voicemail.

My ping app! I plugged Mia's number into the app, and it looked like she was headed toward Blue Ridge Summit on Interstate 16.

She didn't say anything about going anywhere last night.

What the hell is going on?

I rushed to the garage and three cars were parked in there which told me she wasn't driving. Dread fired through me as I ran to the patio. My stomach dropped when I saw the furniture was on its side and the gate was open.

Mia didn't leave willingly.

She was in trouble.

CHAPTER SIXTEEN

"911, CAN I HELP YOU?" the female voice said.

"My friend has been kidnapped. I need you to send the police to Interstate 16 heading toward Blue Ridge Summit. Hang on, I have a license plate number for you," I said in a clear, calm tone.

"Ma'am, can you please tell me what happened. How do you know your friend was kidnapped?"

"If I explain it to you, it will be too late."

With the receiver of Mia's landline in one hand, I pulled up the photo I snapped of Martin's truck from my cell phone. "Please write this down. It's a Pennsylvania plate and it's WBO 425. Did you get that?"

"Yes. What is your name, ma'am?"

Damn it! What was wrong with her? I texted the group chat while I continued, "I am Mia Wallace's neighbor. I spent the night at Mia's house because her husband, Samuel, died. The reading of the will was yesterday, and Samuel didn't leave any money to his sons, Martin and Mason. They threatened her. They told her not to get too comfortable, that this wasn't over. Is any of this starting to get through to you? Mia's sliding glass door was left open."

"I'm sending cops now. While we've been talking, I pulled up the plate number. That vehicle was involved in a hit-and-run last week. What makes you think Mia Wallace was kidnapped?"

"She's not here. And the patio furniture being in disarray shows signs of a struggle. Please. You have to send help. I was with her yesterday when they read the will. Martin and Mason were fuming. They're loose cannons."

"You think they'd hurt her?"

"I think they'll kill her."

"Help is on the way."

A horn blowing diverted my attention to the front window. Catherine was here.

"Ma'am, can you please stay on the line?"

"No. My ride is here."

"What do you mean? Where are you going?"

"To Interstate 16. I have Mia's phone plugged into the ping app. I'm tracking her."

"You need to let the police do their job."

"And risk losing Mia. Hell, no!"

CHAPTER SEVENTEEN

"ARE THEY STILL ON THE interstate?" Catherine asked, driving at top speed.

"Yeah," I replied. "Where could they be taking her?"

"Maryland, maybe?"

"Oh, shit! They turned right and now I lost the tracking."

Catherine nodded. "I bet I know where they're going. Call 911 and tell them to head to High Rock."

"What's High Rock?"

"It's the perfect place to toss someone off a cliff. Hang on!"

Catherine floored her Range Rover while I called the police and told them to go to High Rock. Now we were flying even faster, but it seemed like an eternity since we lost the tracking.

She laid on the horn. "Move it or lose it, buddy! Any sign of the police yet?"

"No. The dispatcher said they're on the way. I don't get it. Where the hell are they?"

"What's the plan if we get there first?"

"You stay in the car. I'll deal with Martin and Mason. They took an instant dislike to me. I'm sure if they see me coming, they'll be distracted and maybe it will give Mia a chance to get away."

"Damn, Bella. You're one brave chick."

Was I being brave or was it the adrenaline pumping through my veins? All those years following true crime, obsessed with someday being on the front lines and stopping the criminals in their tracks was a rush like no other.

Twenty-five minutes had gone by since we lost Mia on the app. Every second that ticked by amped up my heart rate even higher. What if we're too late?

Without warning, Catherine slammed on the brakes and made a sharp right turn down a dirt road.

"Sorry, I almost missed it. Grab onto the — oh, shit — handle. It's about to get bumpy."

I hung on and her car slowed over the uneven terrain. "Are we close?"

"Yeah, it's about a half mile."

"I wonder if you should pull off to the side. We don't want them to hear us coming."

"Okay, I'll stop here. If I go much further there's a big ditch. This way the cops can get through. If they ever show up. Are you sure you don't want me to go with you?"

"No. But do you have anything I can use as a weapon?"

"Bella, I was a girl scout. You bet I do." She reached into her backseat and produced a baseball bat. "This was my daddy's. I call it slugger. Go get 'em."

I clutched onto "slugger" and slid out of the car, careful not to make any noise. When I exhaled, I could see my breath. After I zipped up my hoodie, I looked back at Catherine, and she pointed straight ahead. It had to be where they had Mia. I prayed I wasn't too late.

As the leaves crunched under my feet, my heart thudded. "I can do this," I whispered.

After a few more feet, I spotted Martin and Mason's truck. Mia couldn't be far.

In the distance, I saw them on the highest peak of the cliff, and heard one of them yelling into the void, "I'm the king of the world!"

While they both hooted as if they won the super bowl, they were oblivious to my presence encroaching on their good time.

With the bat perched on my shoulder, I heard a faint cry, "Help... please."

My head snapped to the right, and I found Mia, half-naked, tied to a tree. I bit my lip to keep from crying out in shock. What did they do to her?

"Oh, Mia."

Tears streamed down her face as she trembled. "Th–they... they said they're going to throw me off the cliff up there. They're both wasted. I'm scared. I'm so scared."

I dropped the bat and freed her wrists. "Shh... don't make a sound. I got you."

"H–how did you find me?" she asked in a weak voice.

I took off my hoodie and wrapped it around her waist. "I'll explain later. Come on. We're going to get you out of here."

"What? Who's we?"

I gathered up the clothes Martin and Mason had torn from her body and gave them to her. "Catherine and me. She's not far. You're safe. You're going to be okay."

As we turned to leave, Martin shouted, "Hey! Where do you think you're going?"

I pointed in the direction of Catherine's car. "Mia, run that way. Go!"

She took off, while Martin and Mason stumbled toward me. I grabbed the bat and steadied myself with old slugger at the ready, screaming, "Back off!"

Within seconds, I was flanked by both of them. When Martin reached for the bat, he lost his balance, and face-planted.

Amped with endorphins, I swung and landed a blow right in Mason's stomach. Like lightning, I fled to Catherine's car with the police sirens whirring in the distance.

Out of breath, I opened the car door and hopped in the back. "Catherine, go!"

"Shouldn't we wait? The police are coming," she said.

"And so are Martin and Mason. Lock the doors," I insisted. "Let's get the hell out of here."

Like two drunk zombies, Martin and Mason staggered toward the car.

"Oh, shit!" Catherine exclaimed and somehow managed to whip her Range Rover around before they got to us.

As she drove down the bumpy road, Catherine beeped and waved at the oncoming police car, rolling down her window. "You need to go arrest those two assholes stumbling around before they get away. They're the ones we called about. They kidnapped our friend, Mia, but we got her. She's safe."

The dark-haired officer scratched his scruff. "How in the hell did you manage that?"

"I didn't. Bella Wright did. She's a damn hero."

CHAPTER EIGHTEEN

"ONCE AGAIN, LET'S HEAR IT for Bella," Catherine said and raised a glass. "If I'm ever in a jam, I know who I'll call."

"You were the Thelma to my Louise," I replied. "I couldn't have done it without my co-pilot."

After a sweet weekend with Jack, I found myself the center of attention at a small neighborhood gathering at Catherine's house on Monday evening. Basically, it was our Wine Down Wednesday crew and their husbands. Of course, Julie, Mia, and I went alone since my man was out of town, Julie was divorced, and Mia was once again a widow.

The blonde trio, Catherine's husband, Mick, and Wendy's husband, Lance, were treating me like some sort of a celebrity, but Dave was still as standoffish as ever. The second Dave found me in his garage at the first Wine Down Wednesday, he took an instant dislike to me. Maybe he sensed I knew more about his family than he was comfortable with.

With a shrug and a sip of water, I chose not to give Dave another thought. It was difficult to think at all with Lance's gaze fixed on mine as he approached me.

He raised a glass and winked. "You are quite the heroine. Again, cheers to you."

I lifted my water and replied, "Thanks. Um... where's Wendy?"

"She went to the restroom. By the way, I did eat a piece of the pineapple upside-down cake you made. It was delicious."

"I'll have to give your wife the recipe."

He squeezed my shoulder as he slunk away. "Please do, Bella."

What was it about Lance that made the little hairs on the back of my neck stand up? He seemed to be interested in a lot more than my pineapple upside-down cake.

I shook off the thoughts of Doctor Anderson and put my attention back on Mia. I found her in the same spot where she sat the day of Samuel's funeral.

While everyone was three drinks in, I went to her. "Hey, how are you holding up?"

"Now that I know Mason and Martin are behind bars, I'm doing better."

"When I gave my statement to Sheriff Brady, he said he didn't think they'd be released on bail. They'll be in jail until their trial."

"That's good to hear. I honestly don't know what I would've done without you, Bella. You saved my life. I don't know how I'll ever repay you."

"Just find your joy again. That would make me so happy."

"I'll try. Don't say anything, but I decided to quit seeing Doctor Anderson. After what I've been through, I'd rather talk to a woman. He has an associate in his office named Doctor Heather Perrot. Lance helped me a lot and it was sweet of him to come to Samuel's funeral, but isn't it kind of weird that he's here now?"

"Yeah, you're right. It's super weird."

Mia let out a sigh. "I guess since it's a small town and an even smaller neighborhood, it's bound to happen. When I realized Wendy was married to him, I almost switched therapists. Now I don't want to talk to any men."

"You can talk to me if you want."

"Thank you. I know I've only known you a little while, but you're one of the best friends I've ever had. Sometimes when I close my eyes at night, I can still feel Martin and Mason's hands on me... smell their nasty breath..."

I clasped her hand. "I hope they spend the rest of their days rotting in prison."

Tears flooded her eyes and she nodded.

"You want to get out of here?" I asked.

"Yeah. It was so nice of Catherine to go to all this trouble, but I think I'll head home."

"I'll go with you."

"Bella, you don't have to do that."

"Are you kidding? All of the attention is making me nervous. It's my pleasure."

Together, we did a round of goodbyes to everyone except Dave. It appeared he had already left. Thank God. The man gave me the willies.

After I walked Mia across the street, I stayed on the sidewalk until she flipped on the outside lights.

The fall air smelled like fresh pine with a hint of smoke. Someone must have their wood fireplace burning. It took me back to my first fall with Jack when we attempted camping.

A chuckle escaped as I strolled home. Jack and I were not the outdoorsy type. If it weren't for our own body heat, we would have frozen our asses off. From then on, it was The Four Seasons or bust.

The closer I got to the house, the stronger the smell of smoke became. Did I forget to blow out a candle or something?

By the time I got to my driveway, I realized what the culprit was, or should I say who.

Dave, Nicole's husband, was on my porch, puffing on a cigarette.

"Can I help you with something?" I asked and bristled when my outside lights caught a glimpse of his stern expression.

"I headed out a little early and then I remembered I didn't get a chance to congratulate the hero."

"Oh, well… thanks. I'm allergic to smoke, by the way."

He flicked his cigarette on the ground and moved off the porch to grind it into the cement. "Why does that not surprise me."

Instead of engaging, I clutched onto my keys in the pocket of my sweater and brushed past him.

Dave grabbed me by the elbow.

"What the fuck do you think you're doing?" I snapped. "Let go of me or there's going to be trouble."

He released me and took a step back. "Fine. But just so we're clear, I don't think you're some kind of hero. I can't put my finger on it, Bella Wright. Hmm...Why do I get the feeling there's more to you than meets the eye?"

"The feeling is mutual."

"Just stay away from my family. I don't want you butting your nose into my business."

"Shouldn't you be thanking me?" I asked as my voice rose.

"What the hell is that supposed to mean?"

"Hello, I saved your daughter Emily from an online predator. Remember?"

"What the hell are you talking about?"

"Nicole came to me with concerns about some guy your daughter was talking to on Instagram... I–I thought you knew."

Dave glanced to the heavens as if he was saying, what the fuck! When he exhaled, I thought steam would come out of his ears. "God Damn it," he grumbled.

What did I just do? The last thing I wanted was to put Nicole in a bad place with her ill-tempered husband.

"Uh... look. It was no big deal. Nicole said she'd have Emily block the fake account. She probably didn't want to bother you with female angst. You know, it was girl stuff. I was happy to help."

"You think you're some kind of detective or something?"

"No, I'm just a boring housewife with too much time on her hands."

"A housewife whose husband is never home."

"My husband comes home on the weekends. I'm surprised you haven't seen him jogging in the neighborhood."

"I'll be sure to keep an eye out for him."

"Please do. Be sure to introduce yourself."

"Yeah... I'll do that," he huffed. "So, he's only here a couple days a week. Seems kind of strange if you ask me."

Was he insinuating something tawdry was going on in DC? "I didn't ask you. Now, if you'll excuse me, I'm getting cold. I'm going to head inside."

In a mocking tone, he said, "Well, now, if you'll excuse me, and keep away from my family, I'll head home myself."

"Consider it done."

I rushed into the house and bolted the door behind me. My instinct was to tell Nicole not to go home tonight and let Dave cool off, but I just promised to butt out. My hands were tied.

CHAPTER NINETEEN

"I NEED MORE COFFEE," I mumbled to myself in the kitchen the following morning. I was on no sleep.

After Dave's stern warning last night, I ran upstairs and peeked out the window. He paced in his driveway, smoking one cigarette after another. What did he do to Nicole when she came home? I stood at that window for the better part of an hour before giving up and going to bed.

With the coffee percolating and my nerves on edge, I flinched when the doorbell rang.

To my surprise, it was Wendy with a basket of bagels and a bouquet of gorgeous flowers. Since carbs were my love language, I opened the door.

"Hey, Wendy. Whatcha got there?"

"Oh, just some bagels. The flowers aren't from me. They were sitting on your porch. I thought if you had a second, maybe we could have a chat?"

My heart fluttered with excitement as I grabbed the gorgeous arrangement of purple roses in the crystal vase. "Sure. Your timing is perfect. I'm making coffee. Come on in."

"Thanks," she replied and followed me to the kitchen. "I also have low-fat cream cheese. I hope that's okay."

After placing the flowers on the island, I grabbed an extra mug and some of my everyday china. "That sounds great. Have a seat."

"So, I take it the flowers are from your husband?"

I took a quick peek at the card and grinned. "Yes. After all these years, Jack is so romantic. Purple roses are my favorite, but I'm running out of room in my cupboards to store these pretty vases."

"That's wonderful. Lance hasn't done anything romantic in ages," Wendy replied in a melancholy tone.

"I'm sorry."

"It's okay… uh… I love your kitchen," she said as she took a seat. "It's huge. It really makes the house."

"Thanks, I love it too. I spend most of my time here or in the TV room. It was off to your right when you came inside."

"Yeah, I noticed it. I love the big bay window and how cozy it looks in there."

"That's sweet of you to say," I responded, as I got her some coffee and set it down for her. "What do you take in it?"

"Unless you have milk, I like it black. Promise you won't tell the pumpkin spice latte twins."

I chuckled, placing some silverware and napkins on the table and taking a seat. "I promise your secret is safe with me. I'm sorry I don't have milk."

"No worries. When you're a mom, milk and cereal are staples. It's the only thing my kid will eat in the morning."

I blew past her comment about milk and cereal and got right to the point. "So… what brings you by? Something tells me it's not only my black coffee."

She took a sip and glanced at the flowers. "It's not. I was kind of wondering if I could hire you?"

"Hire me?"

"Remember the night we met? I told you I had a feeling my husband, Lance, was cheating on me."

"Oh, yes. I remember. You know, I'm kind of a people watcher, I like to observe, and I have to say, I think your husband is madly in love with you."

I hated lying to Wendy, but what else could I say? She was a gentle soul who deserved better. Plus, could she handle the truth about her slithery husband?

My first interaction with Lance was strange, my second at Catherine's party, I noticed him checking me out almost the entire time. It was hard not to notice a six-foot, blonde, well-built man giving me a once-over, but my mind drifted back to what Jack said about not getting involved.

"You really think so?" Wendy asked. "He mentioned talking to you at Catherine's. You left quite an impression. It actually made me jealous. He doesn't look at me the same way he used to before we had our son. It's like, I'm a mom now and not a desirable woman anymore."

"Well, what's he like when he comes home from work? Have you ever tried anything romantic? I know it's tough with a kid in the house, but maybe he could spend the weekend at a friend's place. Just try it. Maybe the spark will come back and you'll both feel more reconnected."

"Yeah, that's a great idea. I could do it this weekend. When Lance gets home from work, he goes to his den with a scotch to unwind. I try to be understanding. He's so caring and wonderful to his patients. Sometimes there isn't anything left for me."

After a quick bite of the sesame bagel, I said, "It kind of sounds like you married a great man. He's just being spread a little thin."

Wendy picked up her bagel and put it back down. "Speaking of thin, I was a size two before I had Spencer, our eleven-year-old. Try as I might, I can't get down to that size again. I shouldn't be eating this bagel."

"You look amazing. You're so tiny. Please eat."

She took a huge bite. "Damn, I haven't had anything this decadent in ages. I usually save up my calories and drink them in the evening."

"I tend to eat all my calories before five."

"Is that why you never have wine?"

I shrugged. "I guess. It's not my thing. Please don't tell the Chardonnay twins I said that."

Wendy giggled and took another sip of her plain, black coffee. "I promise. Can I ask you another question?"

"Of course. Anything."

"I was wondering how you found Mia so quickly when you suspected something was wrong. What's your investigating secret?"

"Honestly, if it wasn't for Catherine, we wouldn't have found her. I used an app called Ping. I put her cell phone number in there and it tracked her. She must've had her cell phone in her pocket, or it wouldn't have worked. So, I got lucky. But at one point, we lost her, and Catherine is the one that figured out where they were taking her."

I could almost see her wheels turning when she grabbed her phone. "Okay, I'm not saying I'm officially hiring you, but I am texting you Lance's cell number. I'm going to try your idea this weekend, but if I don't notice any improvement, maybe I'll hire you then? Does that work?"

"Sure. That works," I replied, even though I had no intention of getting involved.

With gusto, she polished off the rest of her bagel and hopped up from her seat. "Well, I hate to eat and run, but I have to go. Spencer forgot his lunch this morning and I need to drop it off before noon."

"That's cool. Let me walk you out."

"Thanks," she said as she hightailed it down the hallway, before stopping at the front room. "Huh... you don't have any pictures up."

"No? I do. I bought that watering can painting at an art show right before we moved."

"I mean, you don't have any photos of you and your husband. I'd love to see what your mystery man looks like. We have wedding pictures plastered all over the house."

"Oh, well, we didn't have much money then, so it was a simple, civil ceremony. I have honeymoon pictures in a photo album upstairs somewhere."

"I'd love the full tour."

"Didn't you say you had to take your son his lunch?"

"Oh, right. Some other time."

After I opened the door, she stepped onto the porch.

"Thanks for stopping by, Wendy. I guess I'll see you tomorrow night at Wine Down Wednesday?"

Maybe I could slip in the backdoor and avoid creepy Dave.

A strange expression formed on her face. "Didn't you get a text from Nicole this morning in the group chat?"

"No. I guess I missed it. What's going on?"

"Wine Down Wednesday is canceled. Nicole took a spill down the stairs last night and sprained her wrist. Poor thing. She's going to lay low for a couple of days. Got to run. Thanks again for the advice. I feel better already."

A spill down the stairs? My gut told me Nicole didn't fall… she was pushed.

CHAPTER TWENTY

BY WEDNESDAY, INSOMNIA WAS KICKING my ass. Obsessed with what happened between Dave, Nicole, and her sprained wrist, I hadn't slept a wink.

Why did all my worries work the graveyard shift? My mind magnified every scenario to the point of paranoia.

Perched at the upstairs bedroom window, I watched and waited for Dave to drive away and then jumped into action.

I zipped up my thickest hoodie and grabbed the turkey wraps I bought for Nicole.

As I rushed to her house, it dawned on me that she might not be happy to see me. Did my unpleasant exchange with Dave lead to her sprained wrist? Did they fight? Did he push her? I knew I wouldn't rest until I found out.

When her front door swung open, I was greeted with the stink eye via Emily Eeyore. "What are you doing here?" she huffed.

"Oh, hey, Emily. I heard about your mom's wrist, and I thought I'd drop by with some food."

With widening eyes, she asked, "What is it?"

"I picked up some turkey wraps and sliced them into smaller servings. I figured it would be easier for your mom to manage."

She furrowed her brow while weighing how appealing the wraps were to her. "Yeah, okay. Come on in. She's watching TV in the back room."

Emily headed left as I made my way to the kitchen. After I placed the wraps in the fridge, I called, "Nicole! Emily let me in."

"Bella? I'm in here."

I stifled my reaction when I spotted her on the couch. Nicole appeared broken and disheveled.

Her stringy blonde locks needed a wash, and she wasn't wearing a stitch of makeup.

"Hi," she said in a quiet tone.

"Hey," I replied. "I'm so sorry about your wrist. How are you feeling?"

"Okay, as long as the Oxycodone holds out."

"I brought you some turkey wraps. I cut them up into smaller pieces so you could manage."

"Thanks. I guess we're canceling Wine Down Wednesday tonight because of me."

"That's okay. I was wondering... um... could we talk for a second?"

"Sure," she replied, sat up, and gestured to the end of the couch. "Did you get the purple roses?"

As I took a seat, I asked, "Yes. How did you know I got roses from my husband?"

"They were delivered to my house by mistake. I asked Emily to put them on your porch. I wanted to make sure they weren't damaged or anything."

"Gotcha... so, I guess Emily knows I was the one that figured out Colin, her Instagram boyfriend, was a fake?"

"Yup. She knows and Dave knows I went to you for help with a private matter."

"Okay, about that. I'm so sorry. I assumed you told him about it. I don't know, your husband makes me nervous. He was standing on my porch when I left Catherine's house."

"These drugs must be stronger than I thought. He was on your porch?"

"Yeah. Dave doesn't like me. I'm not sure why."

"He's always been a little slow to warm up to people. When I started having Wine Down Wednesday, he complained about being the only rooster in the cackling hen house. He softened after a while."

"I think it could be more than that and it's partially my fault."

"What do you mean?"

"The first night I was here, I brought the ice. Dave caught me in the garage putting it in the freezer. I'm pretty sure he thinks I'm some kind of a snoop."

Nicole's eyes darted around the room. "How long were you in the garage?"

"Like two seconds, why do you ask?"

An odd expression formed on her face. "Uh… you know how men are about their garages. I try to avoid going in there. It's like when he opens up my makeup drawer. I don't want him messing up my stuff."

"Yeah, okay. Makes sense."

But did it? What the hell was in the garage? What were they hiding?

"Anyway," I sighed. "I feel terrible for telling Dave I helped you out with the Instagram thing. He seemed kind of angry and then the next thing you know, you've sprained your wrist."

"What's that supposed to mean? Are you implying something?"

"If I was, I want you to know you can trust me. I'm here for you. I swear I'm not a snoop or a gossip. I'm just a friend who has concerns."

Nicole's eyes filled with tears. "I can't… I can't say a word."

"You don't have to. Hey… I'm so sorry."

She hung her head for a moment and collected herself. "The girls, they love him. They think Dave is like a rockstar. Some of this is my fault. We've been going through a rough patch because of me. No one wanted to move once, let alone four times."

"I thought you said you only moved a couple of times."

"Well… I lied to you. Sometimes I feel like my entire life is a lie. One moment. One horrible moment can change everything. I'm probably not making any sense."

"Nicole, believe me, you are. You're making perfect sense to me."

CHAPTER TWENTY-ONE

LATER THAT AFTERNOON MY EYELIDS grew heavy as I fought to stay awake. If I nodded off now, I'd never get any sleep tonight.

Damn, I'm so freaking tired.

While I contemplated the pros and cons of a quick nap, the doorbell rang. With equal parts dread and elation, I slogged my exhausted ass to the door.

Relieved, I opened it up, straight away. "Catherine, hi! What are you up to?"

"Hopefully some girl talk?" She held up a bottle. "I got some Tito's and time on my hands. What do you say?"

"Of course. Come on in."

Once we were settled around the kitchen island with ice-filled tumblers, Catherine cracked open the seal of her vodka. "I can drink it straight if you don't have anything to mix it with."

"Don't be silly," I replied and reached into a cabinet close by, producing the perfect mixer. "Cranberry juice. A friend suggested it."

Catherine laughed with gusto. "Nice. I love it."

"I'm sorry it's not refrigerated."

"That's why God invented ice. Can I mix you up a cocktail?"

I paused, not sure what to say. If I kept refusing alcohol, the neighbors might gossip and wonder what was wrong with me. Not being a big drinker didn't seem to cut it in The Heights.

After I cleared my throat, I said, "Sure. Just a teensy one. I haven't been sleeping very well, I don't want to pass out from exhaustion while you're here."

Catherine chuckled and put a tiny splash in my glass. "I promise, I'll be gentle. I appreciate this. I hate drinking alone. Vodka makes me chatty. If Mick comes home and finds me talking to myself, he might break out a strait jacket."

"Where is Mick?"

"Wednesday is his night out with the guys. You know, usually we have Wine Down Wednesday, but I found myself alone and anxious after a short workday."

"Where's Mia?"

"Didn't you see the group chat? She took off yesterday to visit a friend in California."

"Oh, right," I replied, even though I hadn't checked the group chat.

"I hope Nicole is okay. I called her last night, and she didn't call me back. Have you heard from her?"

While I enjoyed Catherine's company, I knew I couldn't trust her with my suspicions. "No, I haven't. I was going to ask you the same question," I fibbed.

She poured a double shot into her glass and tossed it back. "Whew! Sorry, I just had to take the edge off. Now I can make a proper cocktail."

This time she poured the cranberry juice in first and then filled it to the rim with Tito's. "Cheers!" she said and raised her glass.

I followed suit. "Cheers," I replied taking a small sip, relieved I couldn't even taste the alcohol. It just wasn't my thing. "Um, I'm curious. Since neither of us heard from Nicole, have you seen Dave at the office?"

"Only in passing. I'm mostly with clients showing houses. Why do you ask?"

"Oh, I was wondering if he said anything about how Nicole was doing, that's all."

"Now that you mention it, he didn't. Hmm... I'll ask Mick when he gets home. Maybe Dave said something to him."

"So, Mick and Dave... they get along?"

"Mick can get along with anyone. You've met him. Isn't he great?"

"Yeah, he seems nice. How did you two meet?"

"We met doing a play in college. It was called, 'Star Spangled Girl,' have you heard of it?"

"No, I can't say that I have."

Her chestnut brown eyes lit up. "Well, I was the lead, and Mick and another guy were in it too. The three of us became close and one thing led to another."

I sipped my drink. "How fun and lucky for you."

"What do you mean?"

Wasn't it obvious? "Catherine, you know… aren't most guys that do theatre in college gay?"

She looked like I'd just slapped her, but she recovered quickly and downed her drink. "My parents said the same thing when they met him."

"What do they say now?"

"Nothing. They both passed away."

"I'm so sorry. Mine have too. Would you like another drink or something to eat?"

"Just the booze. The food will only get in the way of my buzz."

As she filled up her glass with more Tito's than cranberry juice, I couldn't help thinking I'd opened up a can of worms I should shut.

Apparently, I was too late. "You know," Catherine said, "I get what you're saying about Mick."

"I swear I wasn't implying anything."

"It's fine. In fact, I'd like to talk about it. Even though we haven't known each other for very long, I trust you, Bella. Out of all the women in the neighborhood, I trust you the most."

Oh, no. Was another secret about to be revealed? I wasn't sure I could keep them all straight.

"Catherine, you don't have to say anything. It's all good."

She tossed back half of her second drink. "No. It's time. It's time I said what is really going on in my marriage."

CHAPTER TWENTY-TWO

THE *DING* OF MY CELL phone in the front room stopped both of us from uttering another syllable.

"I better see who that is," I exclaimed and rushed out of the kitchen.

"It's probably from your husband," Catherine slurred and then went silent.

Instead of Jack saving me from this uncomfortable conversation, it was my brother, Anthony. He was going to swing by on the way to his date with Leigh, the woman he told me about, but she canceled on him.

How sweet of him, I thought as I texted him back. Although Anthony might have to punt Leigh. If my memory was correct, this wasn't the first time she canceled on him. Just as well since she lived in The Heights. My worlds wouldn't collide.

Before I could finish my text to Anthony, the sound of shuffling footsteps drew my attention to the hallway. What the heck?

I put my phone down, followed the noise, and discovered Catherine headed upstairs.

"Catherine? Where are you going?" I asked.

"I'm so sorry," she replied and clutched the banister. "I have an overactive bladder. I was looking for a bathroom."

"Oh! I have a powder room right here," I said and opened the door for her. "It's tucked under the stairs. Most people think it's a closet."

She made her way to the tiny half bath with only a toilet and sink. "Thank you. I'll just be a minute. I would love the grand tour."

"Maybe another time. It's kind of a mess."

After she shut the door, I quickly went to work on a couple of grilled cheese sandwiches for us. If

Catherine was going to keep tossing them back, she needed sustenance.

Once she returned to the kitchen, she freshened her drink. "Whatcha got going on over at the stove?"

"Well, I skipped lunch and was hungry. I'm making us grilled cheese."

"Now that you mention it, I haven't eaten since breakfast. Sounds good."

"What do you normally eat in the morning?"

"Mick made the most wonderful blueberry scones. They were to die for. I don't cook or bake much. He's the one with the culinary skills. Speaking of Mick. I was about to tell you something. It's something I've not shared with anyone."

Please stop talking… please stop talking!

She kept on talking.

"When Mick and I were in college, all we talked about was starting a life together when we graduated. And that's exactly what we did. We got married when we were twenty-three. Time can really fly by. Now we have a twenty-seven-year-old daughter who's married and has a baby of her own."

Redirect the conversation! "Wow! I didn't know you were a grandma. You look so young."

"Oh, stop! I'm in my fifties and going through menopause. I know exactly how I look. Haven't you noticed I'm thicker than the forty-something women in the neighborhood?"

"I mean, you can't compare yourself to them. Julie looks like she hasn't eaten a full meal since the first season of *Game of Thrones* aired."

Catherine threw her head back and laughed. "Oh, my God. That's so funny. I feel like the blonde trinity survive on Altoids and Chardonnay. I used to be just like them when I was their age, but hitting fifty, my parents dying, and going through menopause is a game changer. I've been thin my entire life, and now I gain weight if I smell chocolate."

I put down our sandwiches and joined her at the island. "How do you feel about carbs and cheese?"

"Right now, I say fuck it." She dove in, making yummy noises. "Damn, Bella, this is the best thing I've had in my mouth in a long time."

I took a sip of my drink, hoping she didn't mean what I thought she meant. "I'm glad you like it."

"It's delicious. And it brings me back to Mick. You see, the thing is, we love each other, but our... um... tastes have changed. Sex no longer interests me. I mean, Brad Pitt could walk through the door right now and it wouldn't do a thing for me."

"Whoa. That's saying something. He definitely does it for me. Are you sure it's not a passing phase?"

"I've talked to my doctor and tried a million different things to get through this stage of my life and keep my sex drive from tanking, but I haven't found anything that works for me yet. I guess some women snap back and some don't. Everyone is different. Meanwhile, I have this husband who adores me, but I continue to turn him away."

"I had no idea. I always knew when I got there it wouldn't be a joy ride, but man alive. This sounds rough."

"Savor every moment you have in your forties. It's the greatest decade and you'll miss it when you cross over the big five-o bridge. Ten years ago, Mick and I were still going at it like a couple of teenagers, now... Even if I force myself, nothing happens. At first, I thought, fine, maybe I could be there for him, if you know what I mean. I used to be able to suck the chrome off a bumper and now with the extra weight, I find myself hiding from him."

"What do you mean?" I asked.

"Like when I get undressed. I don't want him to see me naked. And not feeling sexy has put me in a weird headspace. I'm not interested in satisfying him or being intimate in any way."

"Catherine, that's so sad. Are you sure it's only for right now? Maybe in a year you'll feel different?"

"It's possible in a year it might not matter. It's what I've been trying to tell you. I haven't shared this with anyone. Mick... I don't think he's going without sex. I'm pretty sure... uh... he's experimenting... with men."

Why did I have ears? I didn't need to hear about this. It was a private matter. After I collected myself, I said, "I'm sorry. That can't feel very good."

"Why don't you seem more shocked? I thought your jaw would hit the floor."

I sipped my drink. "Um... it's probably the vodka. Alcohol dulls my senses, which is why I don't drink much. It makes me respond differently to things."

She poured another splash of Tito's into my glass. "You're going to need more booze for this conversation. I am too."

Once she emptied her glass, she fixed another cocktail, and I interjected, "Listen, this seems like a delicate situation. Maybe the best thing you could do is talk to Mick about how you're feeling."

"Mick and I talked about this until we were both blue in the face. Communication isn't the problem. I'm the problem. If I hadn't started turning him away, this never would've happened. I should've known he'd be curious about men. Christ, I'm more masculine than he is. Maybe I'm a lesbian?"

"Oh, my," I muttered and chugged my drink. I didn't have the bandwidth for this. What the hell was I supposed to say?

"I'm sorry. You're right, Bella. Maybe I shouldn't be talking about something so private. I've probably said too much."

"No... no... it's fine. I guess I am a little caught off guard, and I'm not sure I can offer any great advice."

"That's okay. It is what it is."

"Do you... do you want a divorce?"

"Oh, hell no. I love him, and I know he loves me. We've been together forever and built a damn fine life. I mean... at least he's not sleeping with another woman. I think that would kill me. Other men? I'm trying to make peace with it. He still comes home to me every night and treats me like a queen. At some point, his libido is going to take a hit too. Then we'll have dinner at four-thirty and watch our programs like Ma and Pa Kettle. I don't want to throw it all away over a few unfortunate years."

I nodded. "There is something to be said for growing old together. Isn't that the dream?"

"Bella, are you tearing up? You look like you're about to cry."

I squeezed my eyes tight and exhaled. "Life is fleeting. I'm sorry. This conversation makes me think about my parents. One passed right after the other. They had a love that was rare."

"Well, that's sweet. I guess it's what everyone wants. I had it and in time I'm sure I will again. Just a rough patch. We'll get through it."

"I have no doubt."

"What about you? What's your story? I talk your ears off all the time and realize I know very little about you. Care to unburden any deep dark secrets?"

"I'm just a boring housewife who battles insomnia. In fact, the vodka has gone right to my head."

"I hear you. I tell you what. I'll leave the bottle and get out of your hair. A little night cap might be what you need to get to sleep. Next time, we'll make it all about you."

What a rare occasion. Someone wanted to know about me. The Heights was filled with chatty women ready to air their dirty laundry without a thought about who they were talking to. Catherine was right. She knew little about me. I intended it to stay that way.

CHAPTER TWENTY-THREE

A FUZZY, FEMALE VOICE SWIRLED around me. "Miss… can I call someone? Are you okay?"

My head pounded while I forced my eyes open. Where the hell was I? An immediate chill swept through my bones when I realized I was on the ground in my backyard. I glanced up at a stranger with big, wild, dark hair. "Who are you?"

"I'm your neighbor, Abby. We share a fence. Um, my dog Brownie was barking, and I came out to see why, and then I saw you. Do you need help?"

"How long have I been out here?"

"I have no clue. It's seven in the morning. You must be freezing. Maybe we should go inside?"

After a giant sigh, I hauled myself upright. "Yeah… my God, you must think I'm crazy. The truth is, I don't know what happened."

Abby gathered up a blanket and an empty Tito's bottle. "Well, as they say, sometimes shit happens. Anyone can have a bad night."

I rubbed my forehead. "It's kind of coming back to me. I had a drink with a friend, but she left and… the rest is kind of… I don't know. I need coffee. Do you want some coffee?"

She seemed hesitant but smiled, and said, "Sure, I have a little time before I need to get to work. Coffee sounds great."

With slow, deliberate steps I made my way to the back porch. Horrified I'd left my screen door hanging wide open and the door leading into the kitchen unlocked.

When we landed inside, empty chip bags littered my countertops. At least it was the snack size.

As my sheer mortification rose, I quickly cleaned up the mess, scrubbed my hands, and grabbed the coffee.

"Thank you," I said in a soft tone. "I really appreciate you coming to my aid. I'd also consider it a personal favor if we kept this between us."

Abby placed the blanket and bottle on the counter. "Of course. It's no one's business."

"Thanks. Uh… have a seat. The coffee will be ready in a second."

As she eased down on one of the chairs around the island, she remarked, "This is a beautiful kitchen. How do you like living in The Heights?"

"It's okay. I've clearly had some good and bad days. Um… by the way, how did you know I lived here and wasn't some random chick who decided to camp outside with a blanket and a bottle of Tito's?"

"Oh… uh… one of your neighbors came into my friend's bookstore on Main Street. Her name is Wendy. She asked me if I was interested in coming to Wine Down Wednesday again and told me I had a new neighbor named Bella with red hair."

While the coffee percolated, I leaned on the counter, still feeling like death. "I am, indeed, Bella with the red hair. Wait, you went to a Wine Down Wednesday?"

"Yeah, only one time. I was in a rough headspace in September. Something terrible happened between my older sister and me. I thought maybe they could be like surrogate big sisters or new friends. I was wrong. It was weird. A lot of one-upping and what they did on their summer vacations. I realized I already had two amazing friends and now they're my sisters. Do you have siblings?"

Wow! She actually asked me a question. "Yeah, a brother, Anthony. We're pretty close. Although, I always wanted a sister."

"Hmm... I used to think I won the lottery when it came to my sister, Amy. The person I thought I knew doesn't exist. Turns out she resented me her entire life for what she went through when we were growing up. Her pretending to be my older, caring sister was all an act."

"I'm so sorry. That's awful," I said as I poured her coffee and set it in front of her. "I haven't lived in The Heights for very long, but I think a lot of people are acting."

She sipped her coffee. "Thanks... uh... what do you mean?"

"Well, take me, for example. To the Wine Down Wednesday crowd, I'm just a boring housewife with a wonderful husband and too much time on my hands. Now you've seen an entirely different Bella this morning. I mean, something like this has never happened to me before, but it doesn't exactly scream citizen of the year."

"Anyone can have an off night. I'm not one to judge."

After I filled my mug and took a drink, I said, "Well, I would. I judge me. The truth is I hardly ever drink, and my friend was over here last night, so I joined her. She was able to toss it back like a pro, but I was being conservative. After she left, I felt kind of anxious and I did a shot of Tito's. It's all kind of hazy after that. I think maybe I heard something out back and that's the last thing I remember. I hadn't slept for days, maybe it was the perfect storm or something."

"Bella, you don't owe me an explanation. Tito's always does me dirty. I think I'm not drunk then, wham, it hits me like a ton of bricks. You probably have a low tolerance. Also, you're kind of tiny."

I rolled my eyes. "I don't feel tiny next to the blondes from Wine Down Wednesday."

"How do you think I felt? I have actual hips and an ass." Abby chuckled. "And my hair has a mind of its own. It defies gravity every morning. My boyfriend said I clogged the drain in the tub."

"Boyfriend? So, the two of you live together?"

"Yeah, I didn't think I would ever do that, but it just kind of worked out that way. Ethan, he's a veterinarian, and I co-own a publishing company. It's still a newish relationship, but he's pretty great. What about you?"

"Me? I've been married for over fifteen years. Jack, my husband, works in DC during the week and is home on the weekends."

"Nice. You have some alone time. If you ever want to come over for dinner some Saturday night, I'd love to have you and your husband at our place."

"That's so nice, I'll be sure to mention it to Jack. He always says he needs time to decompress on the weekends, but you never know."

"Cool. And trust me, I understand what your husband means. Sometimes Ethan will have a rough couple of days at his animal hospital. He never says it directly, but I can tell he needs his quiet time, so I go stay with my friend, Caroline." Abby finished her coffee and said, "Listen, I should let you go. I'm sure you need your alone time as well."

"Um, before you head out. I wanted to ask you something. Do you know who used to live here? I get the feeling there's something strange about the former owner."

Abby glanced down for a moment and cleared her throat. "I haven't lived in Hope Ridge very long, but my friend, Vanessa, was dating the former owner of this house."

"What happened to him?"

She blew out a breath. "He died."

"Was he killed in this house or something?"

"No. Nothing like that. It was a freak accident at High Rock. There's a lot more to the story. You know what, you should read her new book. It's coming out next week. It's called *Missing in Hope Ridge*. It's a fictional version of the deception she experienced last year."

"That sounds right up my alley. I'd love to read her book."

"So, you're a reader?" Abby asked while her eyes lit up with excitement.

"Hmm... mostly I'm a listener. I follow true crime podcasts and blogs, but if your friend's book is based on a true story, I'd love to read it. Thank you for telling me about the previous owner. I had a weird feeling about it, and dreamed up something in my head that was much worse."

"No problem. I work crazy hours, mostly from home, but I go to the bookstore, Turn the Page, a lot. If you ever want to tag along, let me know."

"Considering how you found me this morning, it's an incredibly generous invitation. If I were you, I don't know if I'd be ready to spend more time with the crazy neighbor."

"Listen, this impromptu coffee was ten times more pleasant than my one and only appearance at Wine Down Wednesday. Even on one of your worst days, you're all right with me."

After we said our good-byes, I watched as Abby strolled over to her side of the fence. Maybe I was all right according to her, but I felt all wrong.

I am not okay.

CHAPTER TWENTY-FOUR

"HONEY, I'M HERE." JACK'S SOOTHING voice barely registered. "Hey, are you all right?"

What started out as a headache and mild sore throat after Abby left, morphed into a fever and the sensation of swallowing a hundred razorblades by the next day.

"I think I'm sick," I groaned. "Save yourself."

He chuckled and touched his hand to my forehead. "I'm not going to save myself. I'm staying right here. I'm going to take care of you."

"You're too good to me. I don't deserve you," I whimpered.

"You deserve the moon, baby. Now get some rest. I'll make you some soup."

As I drifted back to sleep, I thought, he didn't know how to make soup, did he?

WHEN MY EYES FLICKERED OPEN, the pounding headache was gone, and I could swallow with more ease.

Jack appeared in the doorway. "Hey, you're up? How's the patient?"

"I think I feel better. How long was I out?"

"Do you remember eating soup?"

"Uh… kind of. It was mostly broth with some carrots floating in it, right?"

He grinned. "Yeah. You complained, but you ate it. That was Friday night. It's Saturday afternoon."

"Wow! I guess I was dead to the world. I hope you don't get sick."

As he approached the bed and hunkered down, his smile faded. "I think I'll be fine. So, do you want to tell me about the bottle of Tito's I found in the bin?"

My stomach clenched. "Um… it's not what it looks like. Catherine, one of our new neighbors, brought it over."

"And she drank an entire bottle by herself?"

"No, I had some, a little, hardly any."

"I thought we agreed that you and alcohol are a bad combination."

Jack was right. Something about my chemical makeup and booze didn't suit. When I went into a deep depression after my parents passed, I used wine like medicine. One glass led to two and the next thing I knew, I was getting black-out drunk.

"We did agree," I mumbled. "And you're totally right. The thing is, I'm starting to feel overwhelmed by my new friends."

"What do you mean?"

"Their lives are not what they seem. Their secrets are a burden to carry. I don't know what it is about me, but these women tell me things they haven't told anyone else. It's a lot."

He reached over and took my hand. "It's because you're kind and an incredible listener."

"Then why don't you ever tell me anything?"

"Honey, I tell you everything. What else do you want to know? I'm an open book."

With a shrug, I let go of his hand and pushed myself upright. "Like your job. All you say is you're stressed out and that you need to decompress. I don't understand why."

"Well, work is the last thing I want to think about when I'm here with you. In general, this has been a tougher transition for me than I thought. I've had trouble with superintendents walking off the job and crews not meeting deadlines. More projects are being tossed in my lap and I'm wearing too many hats. I'm being spread a little thin and I feel like I can't keep up. It was so different at my last job. Everyone did what they were supposed to do. This has been more of a challenge than I thought."

"I had no idea. I'm sorry. I'm glad you told me. It helps me to understand where you're coming from and why you don't want to socialize on the weekend. I wouldn't either."

"Thanks. Do you want to tell me what's going on with the ladies of The Heights?"

I sighed. "I wouldn't know where to start. Oh, I did meet the neighbor that lives behind us. Her name is Abby. She seems super chill and normal. Although, she and her sister had a big falling out. I'd love to find out more about that. She co-owns a publishing company, and her friend owns a bookstore."

"Maybe Abby is the one you should hang out with if the other ladies are being a little too much. Keep in mind, she will probably tell you about her sister."

"That's okay. She didn't say it was a secret or anything. That's what freaks me out. I'm naturally curious, but I don't want to be the only one that knows confidential information."

"Also, you loathe talking about yourself."

"I guess I don't have much to say. No kids, or job. I'm a boring housewife."

"The last thing that you are is boring."

"Would it be okay with you if I went back to therapy?"

"Of course. That's a great idea. Do you have a therapist in mind?"

"Wendy's husband is a therapist and he's been extremely helpful to Mia, but I think it would be weird to go to him. Now that I think about it, Mia changed to a female named Doctor Heather Perrot. She's an associate of Doctor Anderson. I thought maybe I would try to get in to see her. Their office is right on Main Street."

"Sounds perfect. Just like you." He kissed my forehead, rose and headed to the closet.

"Are you going somewhere?"

"Yeah, I was going to head out for a jog."

"Now? It's already getting dark. You know how I feel about that."

"Hey, relax. It's a quiet, peaceful neighborhood. It'll be fine. I'll make it quick."

"Please don't leave," I begged. "Can you stay here with me?"

"What's gotten into you?"

An uneasy sensation flooded my veins, and I couldn't shake it. "I don't know, but I just don't want you to go."

When he put on his running shoes and made his way to the door, my entire being cried out for him, but I couldn't make any sound.

He left…

He was gone…

Loneliness gripped my gut. It was as if he was never coming back.

CHAPTER TWENTY-FIVE

"So, Annabelle, what brings you here today?" Doctor Perrot asked.

"Please, call me Bella. I've been feeling overwhelmed," I replied. "Um, we just moved to Hope Ridge. And it's been tough."

She adjusted her glasses as she gazed directly into my eyes. Doctor Heather Perrot appeared professional in her navy suit and classic, dark blonde bob. She was attractive without being intimidating and had a sympathetic expression as she spoke. "Well, Bella, making friends can be difficult at any age. More so as we get older."

"That's the thing. I'm not struggling to make friends. I have. But these women in my neighborhood… It's as if I'm the Doctor Perrot of my street. It's getting to be too much."

"Can you limit contact with them?"

"Yeah, I guess I should. I don't want to be unkind, but the secrets they tell me and no one else are affecting my life. I don't want to be the only one who knows someone is being abused by their husband."

She shifted in her seat. "Do you know for sure? This could be a matter for the police."

"I don't feel like it's my place to go to the police. She hasn't come right out and said it, but from what I've seen, it's so obvious."

"I can understand how that could affect you. It's a terrible position to be in."

"For some reason, it's triggering the depression I went through when my parents passed away. Everything feels uncertain and scary. I've become irrational with my husband. I flipped out a few nights ago when he went jogging because it was getting dark out."

Jack came back to me. Of course he did. I didn't have anything to worry about, except for my mental health, which was a big deal. All of the secrets had something to do with becoming sick and being sick made me question my stableness. Thank God I could get into Doctor Perrot by Tuesday. Her office on Main Street was easy to find.

"Sometimes when a sense of foreboding occurs it can lead to paranoid thoughts," Doctor Perrot explained. "At least you're aware of what is happening and why you feel the way you do."

"But I don't want to slip back into that dark place. I wasn't myself. What do I do to stop it?"

"First, recognize that even though you feel anxious or low, doesn't mean you're slipping. We can be up one day and down the next without any triggers. Do you have any hobbies? Distracting yourself from a temporary bad headspace can be quite helpful. Exercise is very effective."

"I used to walk a lot while I listen to my favorite podcasts, but now that it's November, it's not always doable with the weather. It gets dark so early too."

"Walking is good. Keeping your focus on other things is excellent. Also, don't beat yourself up if you have a bad day. They happen. Are you on any medications? I'm sorry I didn't get a chance to study your new patient file."

"No, I'm not. They tried a lot of different medications for me in the past. Honestly, I couldn't find the right dosage for any of them. One turned me into a zombie and others made me gain weight, which made me more depressed."

"Unfortunately, a pill can't cure grief. It can help you with symptoms, but the truth is if you lost a loved one you can't take a detour around grief, you have to go through it. There aren't any quick fixes to saying goodbye to those we love the most. It's tough on everyone. You're not alone."

"The truth is I am alone, a lot. My husband works in DC during the week and comes home on weekends. He's wonderful. He's nothing like the husbands in the neighborhood."

"It sounds like you have a lot to be grateful for. That's a wonderful thing to focus on."

"I never thought of it like that. I'm dwelling on the negative instead of the positive. I think I've just had one of those lightbulb moments. Thank you."

"Well, your timing couldn't be more excellent since our session is over. On your way out if you'd like to schedule more sessions, be sure to talk to Debbie. Sometimes the routine of therapy is helpful and sometimes we only need an occasional tune-up. Whatever works for you, Bella."

"Thank you, Doctor Perrot. You've already made a huge difference."

After I left her office, I lingered at the reception desk while Debbie was on the phone. *Should I make another appointment?* A huge weight had already been lifted from my shoulders. I could limit my contact with my new friends. I knew how to shift my focus to something positive. I'd done this work before and hoisted myself out of a dark place.

With confidence, I strolled out of the building and walked toward the square on Main Street. I soldiered on with a renewed appreciation for my situation. Doctor Perrot was right, Jack wasn't anything like the husbands in The Heights, and for that I was grateful.

CHAPTER TWENTY-SIX

LIGHT AS A FEATHER, I journeyed up Main Street looking for the bookstore Abby mentioned. With no wind and warmer temperatures, today was a perfect day to distract myself with a little shopping.

I halted in my tracks when I saw the police station across the street. Should I tell them what I knew about Nicole and Dave? *If you see something, say something.*

No. I'd just committed to limiting contact with my new "friends." I should mind my own business and keep it moving.

When I opened the door to Turn the Page, a little bell jingled. Once inside, I was mesmerized by this charming, magical store. The smell of homemade sugar cookies and cinnamon wrapped around me like a warm hug.

Within seconds, a beautiful, petite, Black woman emerged. "Hi! Welcome to Turn the Page. Can I help you?"

"Hi. Um… I met Abby last week. I live in The Heights, and she told me about this bookstore."

She smiled. "Oh! You must be her new neighbor, Bella?"

"Yes. She told me about a book, *Missing in Hope Ridge*. I wanted to pick up a copy."

Her entire face lit up. "Really? It just came out today! I actually ran out of paperbacks an hour ago."

"Wow! The author must be thrilled."

"I am. I mean, it's me. I'm Vanessa Paige. I own the store."

"Wait, so you're gorgeous and talented? If you can cook too, I might as well off myself right now," I said while a nervous laugh escaped.

"I can cook, but I can't bake. So, there's that."

"Well, congratulations on your book. I was on Main Street, and I thought I'd pop in. Is there another way I can get a copy of it? I'd love to have you sign it."

"Of course. I had no idea I would run out so quickly. My boyfriend was the first one in line to get a copy. Let me shoot him a text. You can have his. I haven't signed it yet."

"You don't have to do that."

"It's no problem. He's just across the street. Give me two seconds. I left my phone in the back."

As Vanessa scurried off, my attention was diverted to the front door when the little bell jingled. My entire being warmed when I saw Abby and an adorable dog coming my way.

"Abby!" I proclaimed. "Is this your dog?"

Landing in front of me, she replied, "Yes. This is Brownie. She's my senior rescue dog."

Brownie was fifty pounds of Heinz 57 cuteness. Was she a shepherd mixed with a boxer and a hundred other things? Who could say? She was definitely a beauty with her large, dark soulful eyes. When she sat for a quick pet, it lifted my spirit.

"Oh my, Brownie, you're a sweetie. And thank you for coming to my rescue last week. You're a life saver."

Abby patted her head. "She literally is. She saved my life one time."

"That's amazing. So, Vanessa ran to the back to text her boyfriend. Um, she seemed to know who I was, and I was wondering…"

She interjected, "I didn't tell her about… you know. I just mentioned I'd met the new neighbor, Bella with red hair, and that you were living in her old boyfriend's house."

"Oh, whew. Thanks. What was her reaction to me living in his house?"

"Uh… I could tell bringing him up upset her a little… you'll understand why after you read her book."

"That's why I came. I wanted to buy her book, but it's sold out."

"There was a line out the door this morning. I was so thrilled for her. It's one of the best debut novels I've ever read."

When Vanessa emerged, grinning from ear to ear, she made a beeline to pet Brownie. "Hey, sweet girl. I haven't seen you in a while."

"I know," Abby responded. "I've been working from home a lot, when I left this morning, she gave me those big, sad eyes, and I knew I had to bring her by. I just popped in to let you know there will be another shipment of books coming first thing in the morning."

"That's great news," Vanessa said. "I'll contact Amanda and have her do a social media blast."

"No need. I'm headed over to her place so Brownie can see Bolt. You relax and enjoy your release day. Celebrate! You deserve it."

"Sorry, Bella," Vanessa asserted. "We're talking business when we should be trying to get to know you better."

"Oh, don't mind me," I replied. "I'm just happy to be out of my neighborhood. Sometimes you can get trapped in your own little bubble. This is a nice change."

"I hope you'll come by more often," Vanessa said. "Although, if you hang out with us too long, we'll end up putting you to work. We could always use more proofreaders at Hope Ridge Publishing if you're interested."

"Really?" I gasped. "That would be wonderful. You have no idea. I was a Philosophy and English major in college."

"That sounds perfect," Abby added. "I'll let you two discuss coming aboard the Hope Ridge Publishing payroll in detail. I'm going to take off so Brownie can get to her play date with Bolt. Congrats again, Vanessa. You're a star."

"None of this would've happened without you," Vanessa responded. "Drive safe."

After Abby and Brownie took off, Vanessa exhaled. "Okay, before I forget, I should have you fill out an application if you're serious about proofreading for us."

"I sure am. Would you mind if I took it with me and filled it out? It will give me an excuse to come back to Main Street."

Vanessa fished out the application from a nearby drawer and placed it in front of me. "Yeah, that works. In fact, I might close up the store a little early tonight anyway. I would like to celebrate with my man."

Before I could say another word, the little bell jingled again. When my focus was on the door this time, my stomach dropped. It was the Sheriff.

Was this a sign I should tell what I knew about Dave and Nicole?

CHAPTER TWENTY-SEVEN

VANESSA NOT ONLY APPEARED UNFAZED by an officer strolling into her store, but she also seemed delighted to see the six-foot, muscle-bound officer with dark brown hair, and piercing blue eyes.

Vanessa greeted him with exuberance. "Hey, Max! There you are. I was just telling my new friend, Bella, I was ready to close early and celebrate."

"Sounds good to me," he replied and placed a book on the counter.

Wait… Vanessa dates the sheriff?

"Thanks for bringing the book," Vanessa said. "I'm going to sign it for Bella. This is Abby's neighbor. Bella, this is Sheriff Max Brady… my boyfriend."

Max studied me. "Nice to meet you. Uh… you look familiar. Have we already met?"

"Only briefly," I responded. "I was the one that called 911 when Mia Wallace was kidnapped. I tracked her phone… and your patrol car and Catherine's Range Rover crossed paths at High Rock. I gave you a statement."

He nodded. "Yeah. Okay. I remember you. I couldn't figure out if you were the bravest woman I ever met or just plum crazy."

I shrugged. "Probably a little of each."

He chuckled. "Well, you did a good thing that day. You saved Mia Wallace's life. If you ever wanted to go into law enforcement, you have my support."

Vanessa put her hands on her hips. "Now, settle down there, Sheriff Brady. Don't poach our new proofreader."

Max grinned. "Whatever you say. I definitely don't want to get in trouble with any of the ladies who run

Hope Ridge Publishing. Now, if you'll excuse me, Bella, I need to head back to the station."

When he captured my gaze, tiny beads of sweat formed on the back of my neck. Should I tell him what I knew about Nicole and Dave? What if I was wrong? What if I made things worse for her?

"Bella… you all right?" Max asked. "You look like you want to say something."

My mouth went dry, and my heart pounded. "Uh… no… I… I just wanted to say thank you for giving up your copy of Vanessa's book. Um… I should head home."

Vanessa wasted no time signing *Missing in Hope Ridge* and sliding the book toward me. "Here you go, Bella."

"Thank you so much. The cover is haunting and beautiful. What do I owe you?"

"Nothing. This one is on the house," Vanessa said.

"Are you sure?"

"Absolutely. Happy reading."

As I turned to leave with my book, Vanessa stopped me. "Aren't you forgetting something?"

"Huh?" I asked, confused.

"The application," Vanessa replied. "You said you were going to take it with you."

I grabbed it off the counter. "Right. Yes. Thank you. I'll see you soon."

After a clumsy goodbye, I rushed out of the store with my book and application. My insides trembled at the thought of Sheriff Brady. Did he know how conflicted I was about Dave and Nicole? It was as if he saw right through me.

Before I could catch my breath, I spied something I wished I hadn't. Coming out of the restaurant next to the bookstore, Lance, Wendy's husband, was engaged in an intimate embrace with Doctor Heather Perrot.

Oh, for crying out loud! Get a room.

Was he wiping away a tear from her cheek?

When they got in separate cars, pulled out onto Main Street, and headed in the same direction, something inside me snapped.

Should I mind my own business? Yes! Should I limit contact with people in my neighborhood? Yes! Did I have any intention of doing either right now? Hell no!

CHAPTER TWENTY-EIGHT

QUICK AS A CAT, I raced down the street, hopped in my car, and punched in Lance's cell number into the Ping app.

Once I saw he was headed toward The Heights, I pulled out onto Main Street and attempted to catch up to Lance without breaking the speed limit.

Luck was on my side. Within a couple of lights, I managed to be two cars behind his grey Audi.

Just like when we were in hot pursuit of Mia, adrenaline fired through me. This was next-level exhilaration. At one point, I nearly got stuck at another red light but slid through in the nick of time.

What in God's name was happening? Doctor Perrot's car turned right, and Lance maintained his way toward our neighborhood. Was I wrong? Did I witness a moment of genuine friendship and not a forbidden dalliance?

I chastised myself the rest of the way home. What the hell was wrong with me? My instincts were way off base. Or were they?

Lance drove past the entrance of The Heights. He wasn't headed home, so I kept following him. Where was he going?

It's none of my business.

And yet, I continued to track him.

It wasn't long before I was in Blue Ridge Summit, and when Lance hung a left into the parking lot of the Hill Top Inn, I swung a right at the gas station across the street.

With casual strides, he made his way to a white Mercedes already parked a few cars away.

When the woman got out of the Mercedes, I gasped. *Holy shit!* There was no doubt Lance was having an affair and who it was with.

I knew the truth, and I could never tell a soul.

CHAPTER TWENTY-NINE

EARLY WEDNESDAY MORNING MY CELL woke me out of a dead sleep. After fumbling for it on the nightstand, I answered, "Hello?"

"Bella? Did I wake you?" Catherine asked.

I'd been dodging her calls since the night of Tito's, now there was no escape. "Uh, yeah. I guess I slept in."

"I'm so sorry. I thought you were an early bird like me."

"Normally, I am… but… anyway… what's up?"

"Well, I feel like you've been avoiding me."

I cleared my throat and sat up. "No. Not at all. I texted you, remember? I let you know I got sick. My husband had to take care of me while he was here over the weekend. I didn't leave the house until yesterday. It's not you, it's me."

I lied. It was her. It was all of them.

"Okay," Catherine replied. "I feel so much better, and I have a huge favor to ask you."

"Um… all right. Go for it."

"It's about Wine Down Wednesday. I said yes to hosting it before I realized Nicole was out of town and Mia might not be home from her trip yet. Please don't leave me alone at my house with Julie and Wendy. It's like hanging out with dumb and dumber."

I chuckled. "Um, you know, I think I'm busy tonight."

"What? You can't be busy. You don't have a job and your husband is in DC. What could possibly be more important than rescuing me from those two blonde nitwits? I'm so desperate for back up, I invited our twenty-five-year-old receptionist, Colleen."

"Then you have back up."

"No, I don't. She says she's busy. What are you doing that is so important you can't throw me a bone?"

Damn it! I couldn't think of one valid excuse. "Okay. I'll come, but I have to be honest. I can't drink. Alcohol and I are not friends. It's just the way it is. So, now you know I'm even a more boring housewife than you thought."

"Oh, hon, I don't think you're boring. I think you're the smart one. Out of all of us living in The Heights, you have it figured out."

"What do you mean?"

"This thing called life. You're the only one who seems to have it all. The rest of us are just pretending and hiding behind our secrets."

This dull housewife had a few secrets of her own.

CHAPTER THIRTY

WITH TREPIDATION AND A KNOT in my stomach, I knocked on Catherine's door for Wine Down Wednesday.

How was I going to look Wendy in the eye, knowing her husband was having an affair with someone? I made a vow to myself that I'd keep this mystery in my vault forever. No good would come from telling the truth.

When Catherine greeted me, she glowed. "Hey, hon, I'm so glad you're here. Come on in."

By design, I arrived early and crossed my fingers and toes that Mia would show up too. "So, how many are you expecting?" I asked as I followed her to the kitchen.

"Mia texted me from the airport. She landed about an hour ago and is on her way here from BWI."

"Awesome. It will be great to see her."

"Yeah. Apparently, she had a wonderful time and thinks she might pack up and head west."

"Well, if anyone deserves a fresh start, it's her."

"A new beginning is a wonderful thing," she replied with a giggle.

"Okay, I have to ask. What is going on with you today? You look all sparkly."

She struck a pose. "Oh, do I? Maybe because I have that post-sex glow."

My mouth gaped open. "What? You and Mick? You guys are back on track?"

She grinned. "Yes. And I have you to thank. After I talked to you last week, it made me realize, I have to fight for my marriage. I can't give up and resign from my sex life. It's not fair to either one of us. So, I went online and found this lube and it gets you jazzed in all the right places. This morning before work, right after I talked to you, I tried it and went to Mick and said, 'Listen, our anniversary is coming up. I don't want to drift apart like two old farts. We're going to the bedroom and my man is going to have his way with me.' And boy did he!"

"Wow! I'm so happy for you, although, I don't think I had anything to do with it."

"Of course you did. If I hadn't felt comfortable enough to divulge my deep dark secret to you, I don't think I would've even tried to get our sex life back. We were stuck in neutral. For some reason, saying it out loud made me take a hard look at myself. Thank you. I owe you one."

"You don't owe me anything. I'm thrilled for you. So, what about Mick and experimenting with men? Did you guys talk about that?"

"We did. We had the most honest conversation we've had in a long time. He told me he had plenty of options available to him, but at the end of the day, he loved me so much, that he couldn't go there. And the guys he hangs out with have been good friends for years, and he didn't want to ruin what he had with them either. I mean, sex just complicates things, unless it's the kind of mind-blowing sex I had this morning."

"So, he's still going to hang out with his friends?"

"Oh, sure. And that is fine with me. This entire time I've been assuming the worst about his Wednesday nights with the guys and the truth is I've had nothing to worry about. I feel twenty pounds lighter even if I'm not."

"You are gorgeous. Sexed-up Catherine agrees with you. By the way, where did Nicole go?"

"You never check our group text, do you?"

I shrugged. "Guilty. It's mostly Julie talking about herself."

She let out a hearty laugh. "Oh, God, you're right. She does prattle on. Anyway, Nicole is visiting her mother in Pittsburgh."

"Nicole's from Pittsburgh? She never mentioned it."

"That's odd. She talked to me about it several times. Honestly, I think Dave misses living there. He worked at Three Rivers Stadium and used to get free tickets to everything."

"Huh... Pittsburgh," I mumbled.

"What's wrong, Bella? You look like you've seen a ghost."

On the contrary, the information provided me with an interesting piece of a puzzle.

CHAPTER THIRTY-ONE

"AND THEN, MY CYCLE INSTRUCTOR told me, for a tiny person with zero percent body fat," Julie bragged, "I had the best ass in class!"

An hour later, everyone was on their third cocktail, and I withered like a wall flower. Too many things zoomed through my mind at once to follow the conversations. The only reason I hadn't left yet was because I was hoping to see Mia.

After a lull in the conversation, I edged my way into the chat. "Wendy, how are things going with you?"

She batted her new, fake, fluffy eye lashes. "Everything is going great, and I have you to thank for it. I've been meaning to stop by or call, but I've just been swamped."

"What did I do?" I asked.

"Remember the great advice you gave me about Lance? Things have been more romantic than ever. And the late nights at the office have dwindled. I mean, with the exception of last night and a few others, but that's due to his associate, Doctor Perrot. Her mother is in hospice care. Lance has really been there for her."

Why didn't I keep my mouth shut?

Julie rolled her eyes. "I hope it stays that way now that you know who is coming back to town. Wendy, wake up and smell the latte. The only reason Lance has been more attentive is because Mia's been in California."

My insides burned and I chastised myself for opening this can of worms. I glanced at Catherine to see if she was going to step in and defend Mia, and she backed out of the room as if she'd just cut one. *Coward!*

Wendy hadn't noticed as she exclaimed, "Julie, I know my husband. He's one hundred percent committed to our family. And, I get it, I've been a little all over the place this last year and worried about our marriage, but I'm telling you, it's good now. Why can't you be happy for me?"

"It's not that I'm not happy for you," Julie replied. "It's that I don't want to see you get hurt again. Don't forget who has been there for you the most and held your hand. I'm telling you, the second that gold-digging whore is back, you will be having those same worries. You need to stay vigilant and keep an eye on her."

It took everything in me to not explode. How dare Julie! While their back and forth continued, I faintly remember hearing the doorbell, before I tried to grab the reins of this horse that was already out of the barn and headed south.

"Julie, you have to stop," I asserted. "Mia is a good person. These wild accusations are beneath you."

With purpose, she rose from her seat and stared me down. "Listen, you're new around here, so back off. I'm being a good friend to Wendy by stating hard facts. What are you doing? Filling her head with romantic delusions?"

Now I was the one rising out of my chair, fuming. "You want hard facts? Mia isn't sleeping with Wendy's husband. That's a fact."

Julie glared at me with pure venom dripping from her lips. "Mia is gutter trash and a goddamn slut. Everyone knows it."

"Oh, my God," Mia gasped by the entry way of the room standing next to Catherine. "What the hell is going on?"

The look on Mia's face broke my heart and infuriated me at the same time. To hell with the vow I made to myself.

This ends now!

With my heart thudding, I spoke the truth. "I'll tell you what's been going on, Mia. Julie has been spreading lies behind your back and Catherine stood by and did nothing, so I'm going to. Here's the damn truth, Wendy. Mia isn't sleeping with your husband, but someone is. I saw them with my own eyes yesterday."

"You don't know what you're talking about," Julie sniped. "Wendy just told you Lance was with his associate and that's why he came home late last night."

"Yeah, except I saw Lance with that associate outside of a restaurant. So, I followed them. Wendy gave me Lance's cell number and I tracked him all the way to Blue Ridge Summit. His associate was following him for a few miles and then made a right turn. Lance didn't stop until he pulled into the parking lot of the Hill Top Inn. Looks like a cute, out-of-the-way place for an affair."

"What do you mean?" Wendy said in a quiet tone as tears flooded her eyes.

"I mean, you've been gaslighted into thinking Mia was the other woman. Pretty ingenious and manipulative plan. The real woman backs off while Mia is out of town, so when Mia comes back, she starts sleeping with your husband on a regular basis, and you'd naturally point the finger at Mia again."

"Just shut up, Bella," Julie huffed. "You're talking crazy."

When Julie said the word crazy, it hit me sideways like a two-by-four to the back of the head. My entire being grew so enraged, I yelled, "Wendy, Julie is the one sleeping with Lance. It's not Mia. I saw Julie yesterday in that parking lot getting out of her white Mercedes and into the arms of your husband. Look at the woman standing in front of you. Look at her and stop blaming Mia. It's Julie, your best friend, your confidant. She's the trash, and someone needs to take her out!"

Everyone froze. No one said a word. They all stared at me with disgust in their eyes. All of the sudden, I was the bad guy, so I left, and I didn't care if I ever saw these women ever again.

CHAPTER THIRTY-TWO

"IT'S A WHOLE MESS," I said to Jack at the dining room table on Friday night. "I opened my mouth and now everyone wants to shoot the messenger."

Jack sipped his red wine. "Even Mia? You stood up for her when no one else would."

"I know. I thought she would at least follow me out of Catherine's or reach out yesterday. I became so manic, I spent all day staring at my phone waiting for someone to text. When they didn't, I decided to block them. I can't keep looking for a lifeline in this group when there isn't one. My anxiety has been through the roof since I spilled the beans on Lance and Julie and scorched the earth. I should've never followed Lance's car."

He raised an eyebrow while he cut into his filet. "I do believe someone said not to get involved."

"You were right. I was a fool not to listen to you. I hope you're not upset with me."

Jack offered a sweet smile, before popping another piece of steak into his mouth. "Upset isn't the right word. I'm a little disappointed, but the filet, roasted potatoes, and my favorite wine is taking the sting out of that. Well played, Mrs. Wright."

I nudged the food around on my plate. "Hey, at least my instincts about Lance weren't completely off base. Any chance I could have a sip of wine?"

He slid the glass across the table. "Of course. I know it's been a rough couple of days."

The second the cabernet danced on my tongue, I relaxed and snuck a second drink when Jack's focus was on his meat. Maybe I should focus on his "meat" too and forget these "friends" in The Heights.

When I went for a third taste of the wine, Jack was quick to stop me. "Hey, let's not push it. You know you and alcohol are a slippery slope."

I placed it back on his side of the table. "You're right. You're always right, Mister Wright. I don't know how you put up with me."

"I feel like some of this could be avoided if I was home more. If you don't like it here, we'll find a place closer to the city."

"That's the weird part, I do like it here. It's just, now I've been ostracized. What do I do with all the time on my hands?"

"Why don't you come back with me this week? You could take in the sights of DC while I'm at work and we could have dinner together every night."

"I like the sound of that. Maybe some of the fallout from my mic drop moment will die down by the time I come back."

"That's true. So, then it's settled. You'll stay with me at the condo. I think you'll like it. It's got all the amenities you could want."

"Oh, I just remembered something. I don't think I can go with you. I didn't get a chance to tell you that after I saw Doctor Perrot, I stopped into this bookstore, and I hit it off with the owner. She gave me an application for a job. They need proofreaders."

Jack leaned back in his chair. "A job? I don't know about that."

"What do you mean you don't know about that?" I shot back.

"It's just, I work hard to provide you with a great life. And when your parents passed, they left you a sizable inheritance. You don't need to work."

"I know I don't need to. I want to. Please, Jack."

He tossed his napkin on his plate. "This has come completely out of left field. I need a second."

After he tromped off to the kitchen, I sat in silence. I guess this wasn't my week. I'd been pissing everyone off, but I never expected this to be a big deal.

When I heard the back door open and slam shut, I decided to sneak a few more sips of wine. How did we go from a nice dinner to another fight? I always said I'd be a stay-at-home mom if we had kids because Jack preferred it, but we never had any. There was no such thing as a stay-at-home wife, was there?

In the quiet, I cleared the table and cleaned the kitchen.

While Jack sulked outside, I went upstairs and got ready for bed. What should I do now? I was excited to have a little side hustle to occupy my time, especially since I was on the outs with the Wine Down Wednesday crowd. Okay, I was supposed to limit my contact with them, but I'd hoped to stay on friendly terms with Mia.

Why did I bother ever talking? It only led to issues.

When my head hit the pillow, my eye lids grew heavy.

Jack, please come back to me.

Within minutes, he came to bed and reached for my hand. "I'm sorry, honey. If you want the job, take it."

"Only if you really mean it."

"Yeah, I mean it. I just hope it won't get in the way of... of us."

"I'm sure it won't."

"But, don't you see, it already has? You were going to come to DC with me and just like that you aren't because of a job you haven't even started."

"It's only part-time. I'm sure they'll be flexible. I don't want to wait to turn in my application. They'll think I'm a flake. You have your work and I love our time together, but maybe I need something too. It might keep me out of trouble."

He chuckled as he drew me close. "You staying out of trouble? I do like the sound of that."

When I was with Jack, time raced. When I was by myself, it crawled. In the blink of an eye, our weekend was over. And I was alone… again.

CHAPTER THIRTY-THREE

"ACCORDING TO OUR RESEARCH," True Maverick said on the latest episode of her podcast, *"in the US almost three women are killed by an intimate partner every day. Nearly half of all murdered women are killed by their partners. Listeners, from my experience, if a wife suddenly ends up dead, it's always the husband."*

It's always the husband…

That last little nugget of information halted my power walk. When I paused my podcast and looked up, I realized I was in front of Mia's house and there was a for sale sign in her yard.

"Good for you, Mia," I muttered to myself and strolled away.

"Bella! Bella, wait!" a voice called out.

I turned around to find Mia waving her arms. In moments, she was on the sidewalk.

"I'm so glad I caught you," she said. "I tried calling and texting you this weekend."

"You did? Um, to be completely honest, when I didn't hear from anyone on Thursday, I blocked all of you. I felt so terrible about Wednesday night."

"Why should you feel terrible? You were the only one standing up for me or telling the truth. Can you come in for a second?"

"Sure. That would be nice."

As I followed her inside, relief washed over me. At least I had one friend?

Mia's home was much grander than anyone else's in The Heights. Now that it was in packed-up boxes, it seemed larger than life.

"I saw the for-sale sign. Did you find a buyer?" I asked standing in her foyer.

"No. But... I'm out of here. The movers come tomorrow. I have a couple of folding chairs in the kitchen, and I haven't boxed up my coffee maker yet. Would you like a cup?"

"Sure, if you have an extra mug."

"Yup. Come on. There's something I want to tell you."

Intrigued, I went to the kitchen with her and took a seat amongst more boxes. "You're so organized. I'm impressed you were able to get this all done in such a short amount of time."

"Oh, I had help. Catherine was here most of the weekend."

"Huh... I wasn't sure how you two were doing after, you know, Wednesday."

"I was pissed at her for not standing up for me the way you did, but she paid her penance and apologized. I wouldn't have been able to get all this done without her and I didn't want to hire outside help. I have enough trust issues as it is."

"Did you give her the listing on the house?"

"Yeah. Despite everything she showed up for me when Samuel passed. And you did too. Before I leave, I wanted you to know how much our friendship has meant to me. From the second we met, you've been kind, honest, and loyal. When I think about what would've happened the day Martin and Mason kidnapped me. If it weren't for you, I wouldn't be getting a second chance to start over. I'd be dead."

"Catherine was instrumental in finding you. She deserves a lot of the credit."

"I know. That's why I want to ask you a favor."

"Anything. Name it."

"Forgive Catherine. She feels terrible about Wednesday night. She's been beating herself up for not standing up for me or you when Julie went off. Now that I'm leaving, you two need to stick together."

"I don't know, Mia. I think I should limit contact with the women in the neighborhood. I spent all day Thursday waiting for someone to reach out to me. My anxiety and paranoia went into overdrive. I felt like some kind of monster when all I did was stand up for you and tell the truth."

"I was in a terrible place on Thursday. I could barely get out of bed. When I've been in that place before I would call my therapist. But Doctor Perrot wasn't available. Some kind of family emergency. I know I should've reached out to you, but I went inward. I was just trying to survive the day. I did call you on Friday and I would've come over, but I knew your husband was there."

"Thank you for telling me that. I've felt like the outcast of The Heights. Can I ask… what happened after I left on Wednesday night?"

She handed me a cup of coffee and leaned against the kitchen counter. "Oh! You missed it. It was like a cage match between Catherine and Julie. I almost had to call 911."

"Oh, my God! Really? I thought you were going to say Julie and Wendy got into it."

"No. You storming out snapped something in Catherine. First of all, Julie was trying to say it wasn't her that was having the affair with Lance. And Wendy initially believed her, and it made Catherine so mad, she let Julie have it. I had to step in between them. It got nasty. Finally, Wendy put it all together. There were some other obvious clues pointing to Julie. When everything crystallized, Wendy took off in tears. I mean, think about it. She was betrayed by her husband and her best friend. I'm sure it crushed her."

"I don't relish the idea of Wendy being hurt. I intended to take that secret to my grave. It was a bomb with too many casualties, but I couldn't keep my mouth shut. The things Julie said about you were horrible and lies."

"Thank you. They were."

"What happened after Wendy left?"

"Catherine kicked Julie out of her house. You know, when I first met you all, I was most envious of Julie. She seemed to have so much confidence and the gift of gab. She was never friendly toward me, so I have no idea why I aspired to be like her. Now, it seems she's just some narcissistic fraud. And Lance, he was an excellent therapist, but how could he cheat on his wife with her best friend?"

I sipped my coffee. "That's next level. It makes me wonder if Julie was the only one he cheated with?"

"Oh, same."

"I know you said he was a good therapist, but I don't get the best vibe from him. Something's off."

"That's interesting. He's always been nothing but professional with me."

"At least he did right by you. Well, I'm glad I ran into you today. My mind thought the worst about everyone, and I realize maybe I was too quick to block everybody. I'm guessing Wendy could use a friend, a real one."

"And Catherine too. She mentioned she tried to reach you, but like me, she needed a day. Wednesday night was a lot."

"Message received. I will unblock Catherine and Wendy. Sometimes my impulsive nature gets the best of me."

Mia cleared her throat. "There's one person who's been missing in action during this situation… and I need to know that if I tell you something, you'll keep it between us. I haven't even told Catherine. Like you, I thought I should take it to my grave, but since I'm leaving town, maybe I should say something."

"Mia, you can tell me anything. I'm like a vault. You can trust me."

She exhaled. "Good. Because I have to tell someone what I saw. It's about Nicole."

CHAPTER THIRTY-FOUR

WITH WEIGHTED STEPS, MIA PULLED up the other folding chair and took a seat. "Do you remember the party Catherine threw for you after you saved me from Samuel's sons?"

"Of course. It was such a sweet gesture, even if the attention was a little overwhelming."

"Right. We both left early, but before you got there, I saw something I wished I hadn't."

"Is this about Nicole and Dave?"

She squeezed her eyes tight and nodded. "I'm kind of afraid to say this out loud, but I don't think Nicole fell down the stairs and sprained her wrist. I think Dave did it."

All the air left my lungs. "Oh, God. I think so too. What did you see?"

"It was something small. An exchange they had in Catherine's kitchen. He grabbed her by her arm and whispered something in her ear, but it wasn't playful, it seemed threatening. And then we found out she 'fell'? Dave makes my skin crawl. I can't explain it."

"Mine too. I haven't told anyone this, not even my husband, but when I got home the night of the party Dave was waiting for me on my porch. It was so creepy. And I don't know what possessed me to say this to him, but I told him I helped Nicole with this situation on Instagram with Emily. I guess, I thought he knew, and he shouldn't be so rude to me. It turns out he didn't know. He was angry Nicole told me anything about his family. And then, boom... she has a sprained wrist."

"Damn, I'm at a loss for words. I guess my gut instinct wasn't far off?"

"No, Mia. We need to listen to our guts more. Like this trip Nicole took to visit her mom in Pittsburgh.

What does it mean? Is she thinking about leaving him? I would. She needs to be somewhere safe."

"Um, she's back from Pittsburgh. Catherine told me she came home on Saturday."

"Does Catherine know what you saw?" I asked.

"Oh, God, no. Dave works in her real estate office. I couldn't put her in that position. Look, Nicole has never been a big fan of mine, but she was sweet to me when Samuel died. I'd feel terrible if I left town and didn't tell anyone what I saw and then something else happened to her. Please, promise me you'll keep an eye out for her."

Now I knew how Michael Corleone felt in *The Godfather*.

Just when I thought I was out, they pull me back in.

CHAPTER THIRTY-FIVE

"AND, DONE!" I SAID TO myself after completing my application for Hope Ridge Publishing.

Later Monday evening, I distracted myself from my conversation with Mia by filling out the application I'd had for nearly a week.

Was there anything I could do for Nicole tonight? Probably not. I unblocked everyone but Julie and vowed to wait for them to reach out to me. Jack's advice about not getting involved weighed heavily on me, but he was also compassionate. If someone came to me for help, he wouldn't want me to turn them away.

Before I could celebrate the first job application I'd finished in almost twenty years, my cell rang.

"Hello, brother dear," I said when I took his call.

"Hello, sister dear," he replied in a funny tone. "You sound good."

"Well, I feel good. I mean, things with the ladies in my neighborhood have been a little rocky, but I think life is on an upswing. Guess who is applying for a job?"

"Really? That's wonderful news, Anna Banana!"

I chuckled. "You haven't called me that in ages."

"Sorry, I couldn't resist."

"No, I like it. It reminds me of Mom and Dad. You know, back in the day when it was just the four of us."

"Those were simpler times."

"Were you calling to check up on me?" I asked.

"Guilty. What are big brothers for?"

"I'm fine. How are things with you?"

"Uh... I guess I can't complain."

"Did you ever meet up with the woman that kept canceling on you? What was her name?"

"Leigh. Leigh Patterson. Um... no... I've pretty much given up on my love life. Which is fine by me. Work has been insane."

What a relief. From what I remembered, Anthony said Leigh lived somewhere in The Heights. Since I was a better listener than a talker, it was best to keep things that way. What if Anthony spilled personal things about me to Leigh and then she told people in the neighborhood?

"Hopefully, I'll be busy with work too," I said. "I met some new friends, and they own a small publishing company. They need proofreaders. Isn't that exciting? I'll be getting paid to read."

"That sounds right up your alley, sis."

"I know, right? The owner of the bookstore also signed her debut novel for me. She's one of the co-owners of Hope Ridge Publishing too. I can't wait to read her book. I'm going to start it tonight."

"Okay, I'll let you go. There's just one more thing. I wanted to ask you about Thanksgiving. What are your plans?"

"Oh, gosh, I haven't thought that far ahead."

"Well, your one and only nephew is coming home from college. Danny and I were thinking of going to a restaurant. So, the invitation is open for you and..."

My bell rang and I interrupted, "Hold that thought, Anthony. Someone is at my door. I have to run."

"Okay, I'll check back with you in a week or so."

"All right, thanks for checking on me, big brother."

"Bye, Anna Banana."

Whoever was at my door just did me a huge favor. I knew Jack would never want to go to a restaurant on Thanksgiving. After my parents passed, Jack and I kept the holidays to ourselves. I loved Anthony and my nephew, Danny, but going out wasn't going to fly with Jack. Maybe they could come here?

The bell rang again in quick succession. "Coming!"

My heart skipped a beat when I opened the door and saw who was on my porch.

"Nicole? Are you okay?"

"No," she replied in a weak tone. "I have to talk to someone. I need help."

CHAPTER THIRTY-SIX

ONCE WE WERE SETTLED ON the living room sofa, I took a long look at Nicole. There were no marks on her or bandages, but she trembled.

"Whatever is going on, Nicole, you can trust me. I'm here for you."

"I know. That's why I came to you," she said softly. "The truth is, I'm scared. I'm scared for my girls and for me."

"Is it Dave? Is he the one you're afraid of?"

She exhaled. "Yes. Um, I went and stayed with my mom for a while. She knows what's been going on. She knows everything. Mom is well off and she wants me to move in with her and bring the girls too. Things at home are too volatile."

"What exactly do you mean by volatile?"

If I was going out on a limb and getting involved, I had to know details.

"Bella, you know exactly what I mean. These past few years things have escalated. Especially since we moved to Hope Ridge. It's kind of interesting. I've been friends with Julie and Wendy since I moved here and they're so caught up in themselves, they never noticed anything off between Dave and me. But you... you noticed. You cared enough to come over after I sprained my wrist. No one else did. I guess if I'm not providing some sort of social outlet, Wendy and Julie have no interest in me personally. And I hate dumping my problems on you, but I don't have anywhere else to turn."

"Oh, Nicole, I'm so sorry you're going through this. What can I do?"

"Just listening is good. My mom is in her fix-it mode. She never cared for Dave. I suppose all the times I cried and complained didn't help their relationship."

"Your mom is trying to protect you. Can I ask, was Dave always like this?"

She tucked a loose strand of hair behind her ears. "I'm not sure how to answer that."

"It's okay. You don't have to. It's none of my business. How have things been since you've been back from Pittsburgh?"

"Who told you I was in Pittsburgh?" Nicole snapped.

"Catherine mentioned it in passing. I guess Dave said something to her. I didn't know it was a secret. I'm sorry."

"It's not. I'm the one who's sorry. I'm all over the place."

"It's okay. Take your time. Breathe. Whatever you want to tell me or not tell me is fine. I'm not going anywhere."

"Well, Dave will be home around nine. Tonight he has bowling. He's in a league. I don't think he'd like it very much if he knew I was here. I feel terrible saying this, Bella, but he doesn't care for you."

"That's okay. I sort of figured."

"The truth is, Dave has always had a bit of a temper. And he's a big guy, so I always wrote it off as it seeming worse because of his size and deep voice. In a lot of ways I think he resents me because I come from money and according to him my expectations were too high. Growing up I had a certain lifestyle. Even after my parents divorced, I got the best of everything. I wanted to give that to my girls, and I don't see anything wrong with that."

"I don't either. It's not like he didn't know that going in."

Nicole's posture shifted. "Yeah, you're right. I never thought of that. Right out of the gate, our wedding was an over-the-top affair with doves and all the bells and whistles. Looking back, Dave complained the entire time."

"Sounds like he's doing a lot more than complaining now."

She wrapped her arms around herself as if she were cold. "Yeah. I wasn't home very long before he found out that I was planning on taking the girls with me to my mom's. It was my fault. I should've been better about keeping track of my phone. He saw a text message from Mom. Last night when he asked to speak to me in our room, I should've known better than to go up there alone. Emily was in the kitchen. She could've come with me. When I went upstairs, I knew by the look on his face he was angry."

"What happened?" I asked and braced myself for the answer.

As tears filled her eyes, Nicole rose from the couch, pulled up her sweater, and showed me her back.

In horror, I shrieked, "Oh, dear God. You have to go to the police!"

CHAPTER THIRTY-SEVEN

MY REACTION TO THE WELTS on her back caused her to pull her sweater down and collapse on the couch, sobbing.

"I'm scared, Bella. I'm so scared," she cried over and over again.

What else could I do but embrace her and tell her it would be okay, even though I didn't believe that for a second. Nicole was in danger. She had to act fast.

As she composed herself, I fetched her some tissues and got her a drink of water. "Thank you," she heaved, "are you sure you don't have anything stronger than water?"

"I'm sorry. I don't," I replied and settled back down on the couch with her. "I could make you some tea."

She sipped her water. "No, that's okay. I'm definitely aching for some wine, but if Dave smelled it on me when he got home, it would be bad... so bad. Among other things, he thinks I have a drinking problem."

"Well, I've never noticed you tossing back more than any of the other ladies at Wine down Wednesday."

She sighed. "He has his reasons."

I blew past her comment. "Nicole... um... can I ask... has Dave ever hurt your daughters?"

"Oh, no. I don't think he ever would, but then I didn't think he would beat me with a belt either. After Dave pushed me and I sprained my wrist, I guess he thought he shouldn't do anything that couldn't be concealed."

"So, then, you didn't fall down the stairs?"

"Of course not. You knew that. I could see it on your face when you came over the next day."

"Yeah… are the girls home when he gets violent? Do you think they know what's going on?"

"If they know, they aren't saying. Sarah and Emily spend most of their time on the lower level. It's sort of like their own little space and Dave soundproofed it when we moved in. At first, I thought he was doing us a favor because of the loud music the girls like to play, but now I realize he did it to hide the truth. If we're on the top floor and the girls are in the basement, they can't hear anything that's going on."

"Like I said before, I think you have to go to the police."

"Oh, Bella. I can't. If I do that and he finds out, he might kill me."

"I grabbed my cell and clicked on the camera icon. You should at least document it. Let me take a photo. I'll take it with my phone. Dave will never know."

"What good would that do?"

"It's like insurance or documentation. I think it's important."

With reluctance, she rose and pulled up her sweater. After I snapped a few photos, I had her turn her head, so her profile was in a couple of shots too.

"Okay, I think I got it," I said and put my phone away.

She returned to the sofa. "Please don't share those with anyone or tell anybody about tonight. This isn't gossip. It's my screwed-up life."

"Don't worry. I promise I'll never tell a soul in The Heights. This is a safe space."

"Thank you. I feel so lucky to have a friend like you. You're one of a kind."

"No need to thank me. I just want you to be safe. Do you have a plan? What happens now?"

"I'm not sure. Usually after an incident, Dave is so ashamed he treats me well. He's softer and not as quick to anger. My birthday is coming up and I thought maybe I could plan a little trip with just the girls, but it falls on Thanksgiving this year, so that's out. I'm thinking of getting a secret burner phone to communicate with my mom, but I have to wait until she Venmo's me the money. She's never done that before and is trying to figure out the app."

"I can give you the money. How much do you need?"

"I think I can pick one up at Walmart for around fifty bucks."

I hopped up from the couch and grabbed my wallet. "I almost never have cash, but I do have some." I fished out three twenties and handed them to her. "Here. Take this."

"Bella, I couldn't," she protested.

"Please. It's the least I can do. I insist."

With a slight nod and a tear rolling down her cheek, she accepted the money. "I'll pay you back."

"It's not necessary. Whatever it takes to keep you safe."

"Despite everything, I don't want you to think Dave is some kind of a monster."

Was she back peddling? Was she afraid she said too much?

"Um…I'm not sure how to respond to that, Nicole. The most important thing is keeping you out of danger. And the girls too."

Like a nervous jackrabbit, she jumped up from the couch. "What time is it?"

I checked my phone. "It's eight forty-five."

"Damn it. I have to go. Again, thank you. And please, I beg you…"

"I promise I won't say a word to anyone."

In a flash, Nicole was out the door and racing across the street. The second she was out of sight I chastised myself for making a promise I knew I wouldn't keep.

CHAPTER THIRTY-EIGHT

BRIGHT AND EARLY THE NEXT morning, Catherine and I were on the curb saying farewell to Mia.

"Please don't hesitate to call if you need anything," I said and embraced her.

She whispered in my ear. "Like Dorothy says to the Scarecrow in *The Wizard of Oz*, I think I'll miss you most of all."

When I released her, tears welled up in her eyes. "I'll miss you too," I replied, "Text me when you land and promise me, you're going to live your best life. You deserve happiness."

"Thank you. If I could be one-tenth as happy as you are, I'll be slaying it."

"When does your plane get in?" Catherine asked.

"Not until after five o'clock your time. My friend is picking me up. I'm going to stay with her until I find a place and my stuff arrives. I hope you'll both come out and visit?"

"Just try to stop me." Catherine grinned. "I've always wanted to spend a winter in California. I'm sure you won't miss the snow."

Mia's voice trembled. "But I will miss the two of you. You showed up for me when I needed you the most. I won't ever forget it."

Catherine pulled her in for a big bear hug. "Okay, you better get in your Uber, hon, before I start crying."

With that, Mia got in the car, and we stood there like two proud parents waving as the Uber drove away.

"And there she goes," Catherine said.

"Yeah, I'm happy for her. After everything Mia's been through, I hope she takes California by the balls."

Catherine let out a deep, hearty laugh. "Amen, Bella. Go get yours, Mia. I feel like our little bird just flew the coup."

"Same," I replied.

"I have some time before the stores open, would you like to come in for a coffee or something?"

"That's so sweet, but I have a to-do list that I need to get cracking on. What stores are you going to?"

"I'm not a hundred-percent sure. I was thinking of running to the outlets in Gettysburg before my first showing. I accidentally on purpose saw something in Mick's closet."

"Accidentally on purpose? How does that happen?"

"You know… you put the dry cleaning away in your husband's closet and poof! You find a little blue box with a white bow tucked between two sweaters."

"You found a Tiffany box? Oh, that's so exciting!"

"I know, right? We said a month ago we wouldn't be exchanging gifts for our anniversary tomorrow night, but I guess Mick wanted to surprise me now that we're getting our groove back. I just need to find a Tiffany equivalent gift for him. And I have to find it today. Any ideas?"

"Oh, gosh. I think men are so hard to buy for. Jack always says burgers and blow jobs, but you can't exactly put a bow on either of those things."

She chuckled. "Well, maybe I'll put a big red bow on me, but I still need to think of something."

"Where are you guys going?"

"We're staying home and I'm having a chef come in and make us a fancy five-course meal."

"Catherine, I'm so happy for you."

"Thank you, I mean that. You're one of a kind. I don't think I've ever had another female friend so invested in her friends' wellbeing. You listen and give of yourself without expecting anything in return. I promise you next time we get together, it's going to be all about you. I want to hear your stories, how you and Jack met, all of it."

Am I high? I didn't think anyone noticed that about me. "I look forward to it. Maybe come over on Thursday and tell me all about your anniversary."

"If I come over on Thursday, we'll be talking about you."

"That works."

Catherine gazed into my eyes. "Are you feeling okay? Forgive me for saying so, but you look tired. Is everything all right?"

"Oh, I stayed up all night reading a book. It was so good. I couldn't put it down."

"And that's all it is?"

"Of course," I fibbed.

While the part about Vanessa's book was true, the real reason I looked tired was because I couldn't stop thinking about Nicole. The book was meant to distract me, and it did, but I never fell asleep.

After we said our good-byes, I strolled home, in deep thought about Nicole. I contemplated going to the police on her behalf. If God forbid Dave did the unthinkable, I'd never forgive myself for not doing everything I could to help.

When I was nearly home, I saw a woman headed toward me. She was so bundled up, I couldn't tell who it was.

As she got closer, she waved, and I prayed for the sidewalk to open up and swallow me whole.

I was too tired and not nearly caffeinated enough for this conversation. Wendy entered the chat.

CHAPTER THIRTY-NINE

ALL I COULD SEE WAS a fake, overly white smile, and blonde wisps peeking out of her hat. Was she coming toward me to punch me in the face for exposing the truth? I knew I should've worn my thickest scarf this morning.

"Hey, Bella," Wendy said in a chipper tone. "I was just coming to say good-bye to Mia. Catherine texted me last night."

I shrugged. "Hi… you're about ten minutes too late. Her Uber already took her to the airport. Did you really want to wish her well?"

"Of course. Why would you ask me that?"

"It's just… since we met, you allowed Julie to blame Mia for your husband straying. I didn't think you cared."

"Yes, I care. I got sidetracked on my way. That's why I'm late."

"Then… you're not angry with me for telling the truth?"

"No. Not at all. I want to thank you. You did me a favor. Lance and I are going into marriage counseling and Julie is out of our lives for good. She hasn't moved yet, but she put her house on the market."

"Woah, I didn't expect you to say that. I'm happy for you if that's what you want."

"Lance, our family, it's all I've ever wanted. You were right. Julie was trying to gaslight me. I'm not saying Lance is blameless. He certainly has a lot more explaining and making up to do, but at least I'm not worrying and wondering why I felt less than. My gut instincts were right on."

"So… you think Julie was the only one he cheated with?"

"How can you ask me that?" Wendy huffed.

"I'm sorry. I don't know why I said that. I didn't sleep last night.

"That's okay. You do look tired. Are you all right?"

This was the first time Wendy had ever inquired about my wellbeing. I almost didn't know how to respond.

"Um… yeah… I'm fine. I was up all night reading a book. It's my own fault."

"Oh, gotcha. Must've been a good book. Um… if you're free right now, do you want to go get a coffee or something?"

While coffee sounded great, I had to stay on task. Plus, if Wendy had any more secrets to lay on me, I didn't want to hear them. Like a laser, my mind was focused on Nicole and what I should do about the lashes on her back from Dave.

"You know I'd love to get coffee. Lord knows I could use one, but today I'm swamped. I have a to-do list a mile long."

"Okay, I guess I'll go on my own. I stopped by Nicole's this morning and she's out of commission."

The tiny hairs on the back of my neck rose. "What do you mean, out of commission? Is she sick?"

"No. Nothing like that, but I am kind of worried about her. She looked like she'd been crying. I guess she tripped on the way to the bathroom last night. Fell right into the wall. Her shoulder took the worst of it. She had her arm in a homemade sling. I told her we were going to have to tape bubble wrap around her. First her wrist and now this. Just between us, I think she drinks too much. That could explain a lot of her injuries."

As Wendy continued talking a mile a minute, my stomach knotted. Nicole didn't trip. It was Dave. I'd stake my life on it. I guess I should quit wondering what to do and just do it.

It was time to let the police know what was going on in the house across the street.

CHAPTER FORTY

"WHAT CAN I DO FOR you, Miss… uh," Sheriff Brady said, searching for my name.

"It's Bella," I replied.

He scratched the scruffy whiskers on his cheek. "Right. Sorry about that. Do you need something?"

I nodded. "I'd like some advice about a domestic situation."

"Well, unless there's a crime being committed, I don't rightly know if I'm the person you should talk to."

"Assault and battery," I blurted without thinking.

He stiffened his spine. "Now that brings me into the loop. Please take a seat."

I pulled up an old metal chair by his desk and sat down. "I've been debating if I should come here and say anything."

Sheriff Brady perched himself on the edge of the desk. "Better safe than sorry is my motto."

"How does this work? Do I have to fill out a formal report or something?"

"First, tell me your concerns and then we'll take it from there."

"Okay… it's about my neighbor across the street. She shared something with me, something I had suspected, that her husband was abusing her. Recently, she claimed she sprained her wrist when she fell down the stairs. At first, she didn't come right out and say it was her husband, but a couple of nights ago, she did."

"I'm afraid there's not a whole lot I can do from some secondhand information. Now, if you could convince her to come in and give a statement, we'd be getting somewhere."

"What if I told you I had proof?"

He furrowed his brow. "What kind of proof?"

I fished my phone out of my purse, pulled up the photos I took, and handed him my phone. "This. This was what he did a few nights ago."

The sheriff grimaced. "Oh, for the love of Christ. And she said specifically it was her husband?"

"Yes. He did it with a belt. She wants to leave him and go to Pittsburgh to stay with her mother. Her husband, Dave, saw some text messages and lost it."

He shook his head in disgust. "Nothing gets me more riled up than a man putting his hands on a woman, but... unfortunately, this could be any female with blonde hair. It's not solid proof it's your neighbor. Many times women will confide in a friend or even call 911, but when push comes to shove, they retract their statements and don't want to press charges."

"I understand. That's why I was up all night wondering if I should say anything. On the one hand, it's none of my business even though Nicole shared it with me, but on the other hand, if she ended up in the hospital or even worse, I'd never forgive myself."

"You're a good friend. This woman, Nicole, she's lucky to have you."

"I appreciate that, but I feel like I'm not doing anything. I mean, I did give her some cash to buy a burner phone so she could communicate with her mom and me without Dave seeing it. When she left, it seemed like she might have regretted telling me everything. She even said sometimes after an incident, her husband is nicer for a while."

"That's very common in a domestic violence situation. Some refer to it as the honeymoon period. It's a sick cycle if you ask me."

"I agree. My husband and I have had our fair share of arguments, but he's never raised a hand to me. No marriage is perfect, but from what I've seen in The Heights, it makes me feel like one of the lucky ones." I

186

rose. "I'm sorry if I wasted your time, Sheriff. I just didn't know what else to do."

"For what it's worth, Bella, I think you did the right thing. Oh, here's your phone. Good on you for getting some evidence. I just wish the victim could be clearly identified."

When he handed me my phone, something clicked. "Actually, she can." I flipped through the pictures until I got to the one with her profile. "See, that's Nicole Taylor. Does that help?"

"Yeah, it does. Do you think we could get a hard copy of that?"

"Of course. This morning when I was debating about coming to see you, I ran into one of Nicole's other friends. She mentioned Nicole had another 'fall,' and she tripped and fell into the wall. According to her, Nicole was wearing a homemade sling and looked like she'd been crying. That was my sign to say something. And if what you say is true about the honeymoon period, poor Nicole didn't even get that this time. I'm beyond worried about what's going on in her house. Their two daughters live with them, but they're older and mostly stay down on the lower level, which Nicole's husband soundproofed. I'm no expert, but it seems like one thing is leading to another and I'm jumping to the most horrible conclusions in my head. Anyway, thank you for listening."

As I turned to go, the sheriff stopped me. "Hang on a minute. If you have a second, we best get a few things down on the record. What did you say the husband's name was again?"

"It's Dave, Dave Taylor, and I think he's dangerous."

CHAPTER FORTY-ONE

YOU DID THE RIGHT THING. You did the right thing. You did the right thing.

As I crossed the street, I repeated that mantra over and over in my head. A part of me related to Nicole. Once you said things out loud, you couldn't take them back. I didn't just tell the sheriff everything I knew, I put it in writing and turned over my photos. If the police showed up at Nicole's house to question Dave... I shuddered with a queasy sensation burning in my gut.

What have I done?

Like a bright shining beacon, the bookstore, Turn the Page was there. As soon as I walked in a calm came over me.

With a huge smile, Vanessa was there to greet me. "Hi! Bella, right?"

"Yes. You remembered," I replied.

"Of course. How are you doing?"

"Better now that I'm here. Your store has some sort of magical pheromones. I was having an off-day until now."

"Aw... I'm happy to hear that. What can I do for you?"

Before I could answer, a man with brown hair and a medium build strolled into the store on a mission. "Hey, Vanessa, have you seen Abby? I've tried calling her a hundred times. Any chance she's stopping by today?"

"Uh... Jeremy, I'm kind of in the middle of something," Vanessa said in an emphatic tone.

He glanced at me and kept talking as if I wasn't here. "So, Abby? Do you have any idea how to reach her? It's important."

Vanessa cocked her head. "If I see her, I will give her the message, but what we're not going to do is come into my place of business and disrupt things."

She stood her ground and sent this man out of the store with his tail between his legs.

Vanessa sighed. "Lord, give me the strength not to throttle that man. I'm so sorry that happened in front of you, Bella."

"Oh, no need to apologize. Who was that?"

"Abby's brother-in-law, Jeremy. It's a long story."

"Right... you know, Abby mentioned something about her sister and a falling out."

"It was more like the bomb heard around the world. Her sister did her dirty. Sometimes the people who claim to love you the most hurt you the most. I've experienced it myself."

"Yes!" I shouted. "I'm sorry. I said that way too loud. What I mean is, I read your book. I was up all night reading it. I can't believe this is your debut novel. It moved me in ways I can't even describe."

Vanessa beamed. "Oh, my God! Thanks. That means so much to me. I was worried when I didn't get your application back right away, you read the book and were like, no, ma'am, I don't want to work with her."

"No. The exact opposite," I said, as I pulled out the application from my purse, and handed it to her.

She unfolded it with an unusual expression. "Oh... um... I think you spilled something on it. Is that coffee?"

My heart sank in mortification. "Probably... I'm so sorry... I didn't sleep last night and I... I can redo it."

"No. It's okay. Stuff happens. I could've emailed you one and it would've been a lot quicker. Unfortunately, we've filled one of the slots, so as we get a little busier next year, we'll need more people, but for right now, we're set."

I blew it. "Sure. That's fine. The holidays are crazy for me anyway."

"I'll hang onto this if that's okay. It has all of your information. This way if anything changes, we can give you a call."

"That would be great. I can't believe how long it took me to get the application back to you. That's really not like me."

"Are you all right?"

"Uh… yeah. Just a lot going on with the ladies in the neighborhood. You know, drama, drama, drama," I responded, trying to make light of it.

"I get it. From my experience, there's never a dull moment in Hope Ridge."

CHAPTER FORTY-TWO

WHEN I DROVE DOWN MY street, I spotted Dave's truck in the driveway. For a moment I slowed, wondering what he would do to her tonight. Poor Nicole. It made me wonder when the violence in their relationship began. What triggered him and pushed him over the edge? How long had she been walking on eggshells? Were her daughters clueless or did one of them have an inkling?

Once I was inside my house, my mind harkened back to a case from our old neighborhood. I'd been putting my sleuthing skills on the back burner since meeting the women from The Heights. They kept me busy in ways I could've never predicted.

After a shower and a bite to eat, I relaxed in front of my computer, ready to dive in. Because the ladies never asked me any questions, I never told them the facts about where we lived before moving into this house or that I wasn't a real redhead.

Being a great listener had its advantages. When I made a fresh start, I could be anyone from anywhere. The truth was, Jack and I lived in a suburb of Pittsburgh, not Chicago. We had a beautiful home in Mt. Lebanon, eight miles south of downtown Pittsburgh. The tree-lined streets and award-winning school district screamed small-town family life.

When something horrible happened in our community five years ago, people stepped forward to help. As time dragged on and the leads dried up, it became a cold case, and everyone forgot about it. Everyone but me. I would never forget.

With my fingers tapping away on the keyboard of my laptop, I was startled by my ringing cell phone.

"Unknown caller?" I muttered to myself before answering. "Hello?"

"Bella, it's me, Nicole."

"Oh, hi. Are you okay?"

"Yeah, um… I bought the burner phone with the money you gave me because Dave has been checking mine since he saw the text exchange with my mom."

"Good. I ran into Wendy, and she said something about how you tripped and fell into the wall? Is that really what happened?"

"You and I both know it isn't. Dave got home early from bowling and found out I was at your house. He flipped. He said you're not to be trusted. And the fight went on from there."

"Oh, God, Nicole. I'm so sorry."

"Look, I told him you and your husband were the ones fighting and you reached out to me. So, if he asks you about it, I wanted you to know that's what I said."

"Of course. We need to keep you safe. I'm scared for you."

"Don't be. I swear I'm okay."

"How can you say that? You're calling me from a burner phone."

"It just… Dave did a complete turnaround today. For years, the girls have been wanting a cat and he's said no because he's allergic, and tonight he surprised them with their first pet. It was so sweet. He told them he was going to get allergy shots and he told me he wants to start over. They're down on the lower level, so I know they can't hear me."

This was emotional whiplash. "I… uh… I don't know what to say. Um… I'm happy for you?"

"Thank you. I want things to work out. I don't want to lose my family. We've already lost so much."

What did that mean? Not sure how to respond, I simply said, "Family is everything."

"I knew you would understand. Thank you. I've made so many mistakes, and a lot of this is my fault, but now maybe with sweet, little Ambrose, the tabby cat, we could start over. Dave even said he wanted it to just be the four of us for Thanksgiving. A real down-home family holiday and since it's also my birthday, it would be special. The best part is, I don't even have to cook, he already placed an order with Fat Russell's Barbecue."

"That sounds wonderful. I hope this is a new beginning for you."

"Thanks… there's just one more thing…. well, two more things."

"Name it. Anything you need."

"I probably can't hang out with you or anything. I don't want to upset the applecart with Dave. So, if you don't hear from me, don't worry. I'm just trying to keep the peace."

"That's okay. I get it. I don't want to interfere in your reconciliation. What's the other thing?"

"I need you to promise to delete those pictures you took of the lashes on my back. I know you wouldn't show them to anyone, but I can't take any chances. Please destroy them and don't ever tell a soul what I told you about Dave hurting me. No good could come of it, especially for me."

A lump formed in my throat. "Sure, Nicole… whatever you say."

CHAPTER FORTY-THREE

REELING ALL NIGHT, I HADN'T slept a wink. My conversations with Nicole and Sheriff Brady clawed at me. Overwhelmed and exhausted, I sacked out on the sofa for an afternoon nap.

As I drifted off, a pounding on the front door made me bolt upright. Who could that be? I wasn't expecting anyone.

Shuffling to the door, I prayed it wasn't Nicole with a bloody lip. Her reconciliation with Dave couldn't have gone up in smoke already. Right?

When I swung open the door, I was shocked to find Catherine with tear-stained eyes. "Hey, are you okay? Do you want to come in?"

"Please," she cried. "I'm sorry to burst in on you in the middle of the day, but I didn't know where else to turn."

"Don't apologize. Come in."

She followed me to the sofa and plopped down. "I've been a fool, Bella. An absolute fool."

I joined her on the couch. "What are you talking about? The last time I saw you, you were off to buy Mick something for your anniversary because you found the Tiffany box. What happened?"

"Oh, I'll tell you what happened. I went to the outlets, and I bought him a beautiful watch. Thon, I did a couple of showings, rushed home, shaved my legs... above the knee, and squeezed my fat ass into my best lingerie. I threw on some cute lounge wear over it because the chef was there. I figured after dinner Mick could unwrap me like a present, even though the lace on lingerie chaffed my bikini area like a bitch. After dinner, the chef left, and like a kid at Christmas, I ran upstairs and got his new watch."

"Well, that all sounds wonderful."

"There's more. Mick was upset I bought him a gift since he didn't have one for me."

"Wait… but you saw the Tiffany box."

"You're damn right I did. I even practiced my, 'oh, Mick, you shouldn't have' face. But he didn't give me the box. Instead, we got into an argument. And by the end of the night, I was apologizing to him."

"Maybe the jewelry in the Tiffany box is your Christmas present."

"I thought of that too. Mick was up and out of the house early, so I snooped in his closet. I was going to open the box. If it was the diamond tennis bracelet I'd been hinting about since last Christmas, I could deal with that."

"Did you tell him you saw the box?"

"No, I didn't want to ruin his surprise. Only I was the one who was surprised."

"What do you mean?"

"The Tiffany box was gone."

"Wow, that's crazy. Are you sure you saw it in the first place?"

"I'm one-hundred-percent positive."

"What did you do?"

"What could I do?" Catherine huffed. "I got myself dressed and went to work. I figured the mystery of the little blue box with the white, satin bow would sort itself out, or tonight I would just be honest with Mick and tell him I saw it."

"Did you get to the bottom of it?"

She nodded with tears welling up in her eyes. "Yeah. When I got to the office our receptionist, Colleen, the twenty-five-year-old I mentioned… was wearing a diamond tennis bracelet. I asked her if it was new and she said yes, and how she never had anything from Tiffany's before. I felt like Emma Thompson in *Love Actually*. The room began to spin while I put it all together. My husband has been fucking the receptionist right under my nose. A little twenty-five-year-old girl with perky tits and no body fat. Fucking Colleen Hooper looked me right in the face and grinned about a new, expensive bracelet my husband gave her!"

My jaw dropped. "Oh, my God. Oh, Catherine. I can't believe it. What... what did you do? I can't even imagine."

Her voice shook in sorrow. "It was like my life flashed before me in slow motion. My body felt like it was on fire, and I steeled myself from slapping Colleen. Somehow, I plastered a smile on my face while I was raging inside. I can't even remember if I said anything to her, but I excused myself and went to my office and fell apart. And then... I started putting the pieces together. This affair had been going on right in front of me for God knows how long. It tracked. Mick was never out with the guys on Wednesday night, he was with her. This bullshit about possibly being bi-curious was all a ruse."

"I don't know what to say. I'm so sorry."

She wiped her eyes. "I'm sorry too. I'm sorry my husband is no better than Wendy's shitty husband. You know, I thought Wendy was a dumbass from the first time I met her. One look at Lance and you could tell the man was a player. But no. Not my Mick. I always said the man wasn't perfect, but he was perfect for me. I'm such an idiot."

"You're not an idiot. I'm in as much shock as you are. You deserve better. Can I ask what happened after you went into your office?"

"I canceled my showings, and I texted Mick that I needed him to meet me back at the house ASAP. It was an emergency. I left, drove home, and I ransacked his closet. I went a little nuts and threw all of his stuff in garbage bags. By the time he got there, I was in a full rampage. I started breaking shit in his den. I couldn't stop. But you know what the worst part is? He didn't deny the affair with Colleen. He claims he's in love with her. In love with a girl younger than his own daughter. It's disgusting. And he says it's my fault. My fault! That when I turned fifty, I changed. Damn right, I changed. It's literally called the change! What the hell did he expect? He wasn't exactly the same either. It was all I could do to not kill him. That's why I ran to your house, Bella. I was afraid I would murder him. I've never felt this kind of anger and betrayal. He didn't even say he was sorry. He turned the whole thing around on me. You hear those stories about a wife killing a husband or the other way around. I never understood it until today. I snapped and now I'm scared I'll never be the same person I was when I woke up today. That I'm capable of murdering someone. If there had been a gun in my house, I would've shot Mick. There's no doubt in my mind. That scares me."

Catherine's words frightened me to my core. The ugly truth spilling from her soul was something I'd never forget. Sometimes people were pushed to the brink and did things they never imagined were in them. Now Catherine, through no fault of her own, was one of those people.

I did my best to comfort her. "What can I do to help? You're too good of a woman to be treated this way."

She balled her hands into fists. "I appreciate that, but right now I just want to punch him out. That's why I came over here. Breaking a few of his things did nothing to tamp down the storm I feel inside me. Storm is too soft a word. It's more like a violent hurricane."

"You're in a safe space, Catherine. I have a couple of vases if you want to go out back and smash them."

A slight chuckle escaped. "You're amazing, and probably the best friend I've made in years. Thank you.

I just need to let this anger subside before I see Mick again. All those years... and he's tossed me away for someone who probably doesn't even know what albums or records were."

"Or even CDs. Forget about cassette tapes too."

"Or VCRs? Stupid little twit probably came out of the womb Instagram-ready. I asked Colleen one time what she wanted to do, what her hopes and dreams were, and she said, in an annoying baby voice, 'I want to be an influencer, like you know, post stuff about fashion.' I should've sacked her ass then. I hope she's prepared for ironing Mick's shirts every day and making him fresh juice, so he doesn't get constipated. Does Gucci or Prada make a stool softener?"

I bit my lip to keep from laughing. Even in a crisis, she was hilarious. "Um... here's a question... Can you fire her? I know you and Mick own the real estate company, but is there an HR department?"

She straightened her spine and her eyes widened. "Jesus Christ on the cross. Bella, you're brilliant."

"So, you can fire her?"

"No, I won't have to. A light bulb just went off... The business is mine, the house is mine. Everything we own, it's all in my name."

"Are you serious? How did that happen?"

"Well... Mick happened. About twelve years ago we had to file for bankruptcy. I mean, it was bad. Mick is terrible with money. We were living way beyond our means and finally, the bottom fell out of the boat. If it weren't for my parents, we would've been out on the street. My mom, God rest her soul, took me aside and told me to go ahead and file for bankruptcy, and after we got through that, she would give me a little nest egg she'd been saving, but only if I put everything in my name and took over the finances. That's exactly what I did. And when my parents passed, there was another chunk of change for me and only me. He wasn't allowed to touch it. Without me, Mick would be just another real estate agent pounding the pavement. Wait until his sidepiece finds out he doesn't have any money. I don't have to fire Colleen because when I go home tonight, I'm firing Mick."

"Woah, he done pissed off the wrong woman. Good for you, Catherine. I'd contact a lawyer right away and cancel his credit cards too."

"Oh, right. I'm going to do that too. Well... hell's bells, I feel so much better already. Thank you. Suddenly, I'm not mad, I don't have to be. He'll be the one that's pissed off. Let's see how he likes it. I'll tell you what, you should never mess with women over fifty. We know more, we've seen it all, and we're sick of everyone's shit."

"Amen. That's the spirit. You've got this. I'm behind you one hundred percent."

She hopped off the couch with a gleam in her eye. "Thanks. I'm going to run home and put this plan into action. In a few short hours, Mick won't have a pot to piss in or a window to throw it out of. That ought to frost his balls."

I laughed and hauled myself off the couch. "You go, girl... ugh... I'm probably too old to say that."

Catherine clasped my face with both hands. "No, you, my dear friend, you're perfection. Sorry to have an epiphany and run, but this can't wait."

As I followed her rushing to the door, I said, "Jack will be here this weekend, but if you need anything text me."

"Once I get my lawyer on board, I'm sure I'll be fine, but maybe you could come over one night next week. It doesn't have to be Wednesday, whatever works best for you."

"Okay, sounds good. I would like to hear how things are going. It sounds like you're about to rock

Mick's world. Oh, don't forget to change your life insurance policy if you have one."

She halted in her tracks and faced me with a strained expression. "Damn, I never would've thought of that. You're right. If something happens to me between now and before I get that done, you go to the police and tell them what I told you. Promise?"

"Catherine, I'd do anything for you, but you don't think Mick would hurt you, do you? He's nothing like Nicole's husband, Dave."

Her jaw went slack. "What did you say?"

The second it flew out of my mouth, I regretted it. "Oh, nothing."

"You think Dave abuses Nicole, my mild-mannered office manager, Dave?"

"Uh... no... no.... Maybe. I don't know. Just some things I've seen and what Nicole has told me in a roundabout way. Please forget I said anything. I shouldn't have mentioned it. It's just, last week I was listening to this true crime podcast and the host said in her opinion when a wife is murdered, it's always the husband. It's stuck in my head. I probably watch too much Dateline."

I could almost see Catherine's wheels turning as she mumbled, "Huh... It's always the husband."

CHAPTER FORTY-FOUR

"SO, AS YOU CAN IMAGINE, each day that passes by, I've decided, I'm the luckiest wife in the neighborhood, Mister Wright," I said to Jack as I cleared the dinner dishes.

He followed me to the kitchen, carrying the empty pasta bowl. "Just the neighborhood?"

With a chuckle, I faced him. "Okay, all of Hope Ridge."

Jack sat the bowl on the island, closed the gap between us, and grinned like the devil. "Just Hope Ridge?"

I threw my arms around his neck. "No. Not just Hope Ridge. You're the best husband in the entire world. I mean that. I love you, Jack."

He pulled me close. "I love you too, baby. Let's forget about these dishes and go upstairs. I have to have you. Come."

As he took my hand in his and led me upstairs to our bedroom, my skin tingled from head to toe. This was all I needed. The two of us in our own bubble, our sanctuary, our home. Jack was my home, my family, my everything.

While the streets of The Heights were lined with lies, broken dreams, and betrayal, I had a man that would move heaven and earth to give me everything I wanted. Little did he know, he was the only thing I ever wanted, wrapped up in one exquisite package.

He was mine and I was his. Our bond was so strong, nothing could break it. Perfection didn't exist, but as he took me that night, I held onto his broad shoulders, and we moved together in our own sensual harmony.

The passion, the intimacy, and the ecstasy were next level as we climbed toward our intense climax and rode the wave of an orgasm that left me quaking.

His lips met with mine in a kiss so sweet, I would remember it for the rest of my life.

With his forehead resting on mine, he whispered, "I think we both needed that."

"Absolutely," I gasped. "Wow… is there… is there any chance you could stay in Hope Ridge until after Thanksgiving?"

"Honey, you know I would if could," Jack said as he started to pull away.

"Please, don't go," I begged.

"I'll be back on Wednesday night. I promise."

"No, I mean, don't move. Stay inside me."

"Okay, I'm right here. What's wrong? Are you all right?"

The stress of the week bubbled up and spilled down my cheeks. I didn't tell Jack I went to the sheriff about Dave and gave him the pictures of Nicole's back. It was eating me alive to keep secrets from him. I only told him what happened to Catherine. If he had found out I'd gotten involved in such a volatile situation of domestic abuse, he probably wouldn't be holding me like this. Should I say something?

I peeked up at him and said, "I'm… I think I… I'm just looking forward to Thanksgiving, that's all."

"Are you sure that's it? You can tell me anything?"

"I know," I replied and then thought of something else I hadn't mentioned. "It's just Anthony called, and he mentioned him and Danny are going to a restaurant on Thanksgiving and…"

With a huff, Jack moved away from me and interrupted, "Please tell me you didn't say we'd join them."

"No, I didn't commit to anything. Our phone call got cut short. I was going to tell him I was cooking and if they wanted to come later in the day for dessert or something. I thought I'd ask you first. This way he gets some alone time with his son, and you and I get ours."

A silence fell between us. Jack didn't enjoy sharing me, but family was family. When the quiet grew uncomfortable, I said, "You know what, it's fine. I'll call Anthony tomorrow and tell him we have plans, that we got invited to a get-together in the neighborhood or something."

He flopped back on his pillow. "No. Don't do that. I like your idea. It would be good to see them."

Relief swept over me as I reached for him. "Thank you, Jack. I'm sure you get sick of a steady diet of just me."

He yanked me close to him. "Never. A steady diet of you is all I want. You're delicious. In fact, Mrs. Wright… I could eat you up right now."

As I squealed and licked my lips, the sight of his beautiful body was overpowering. "You know, I'm a little hungry too."

"I like the way you think, gorgeous."

CHAPTER FORTY-FIVE

"*DEVON REINHOLD WAS FOUND IN her basement, dead. Detectives were at a loss because her husband, Donald, had an airtight alibi, or did he? Once his alibi began to fold like a cheap tent, authorities discovered a pair of leather gloves buried in the backyard with, you guessed it, Donald's DNA. It turns out, dear listeners, he strangled his wife with his hands, not his bare hands, his leather gloved hands.*"

When I looked down and realized I was wearing Jack's leather gloves, I shuddered. Was it the cold morning air or the strange coincidence of wearing gloves? I shook it off. I'd been stealing Jack's gloves since the early days. Even though they were too big, they seemed warmer to me.

I paused my True Maverick podcast and picked up my pace. I'd gotten so wrapped up in this latest episode, I found myself a bit bewildered. What street was I on? It didn't look familiar to me.

In the distance, I spotted a bundled-up woman and kid getting into their car. Since it was seven a.m. on a Monday morning, she was probably driving him to school. Walking even faster, I thought I'd try to catch her before she pulled away and ask her which direction was Maple Street.

By the time I was close enough to wave, the mom, hopped out of the car and crossed her arms.

Oh, shit! It was Julie.

With her hat, coat and scarf, I didn't figure that out until it was too late.

"Hey, what the hell do you want?" Julie scoffed. "Haven't you done enough?"

"I don't want anything," I replied. "Obviously, you're taking your kid to school, so never mind. Forget you saw me."

"I wish I could forget you and your big mouth."

"Yeah, okay. See you later."

"Wait," she insisted. "I have a few things to say to you."

"What about your kid?"

"He's fine. The heat's on and he has his iPad. But you bring up a good point. What about my kid? Did you know because of you and your giant mouth, we have to move out of this neighborhood, and he'll have to change schools after the holidays."

"I mean, I'm not the one who was sleeping with Wendy's husband. That was all you."

"Fuck you," she shouted.

"Who talks like that? And in front of your kid. It seems to me if you were that concerned about him you wouldn't have had an affair in the first place."

"Oh, sure. I'm the whore with the scarlet letter, but when my husband cheated on me, he got to keep his job, our house, and the slut he was screwing."

"I'm sorry. I didn't know that happened to you."

Julie shoved her hands in her pockets. "Well, now you know. My ex-husband is an ass and when I moved into this neighborhood, Lance was nice to me. I was on my own with no one to help do that crap around the house that husbands do. Believe it or not, I care about Wendy and their son. He was my son's best friend and now it's all ruined. Why couldn't you just butt out?"

"I would've. I never dreamed of telling anyone I saw you two together… but you were nailing Mia to the cross for something she didn't do. I snapped. Mia had been through enough. I couldn't take it. Why did you do that to her?"

"Because… I was trying to buy some more time. Lance was getting ready to leave Wendy. I thought I was getting my second chance at a happy ending. Now everything is a mess. Lance has blocked me. I'm like the pariah of the neighborhood and I have you to thank."

I shrugged. "You're welcome."

What little I could see of her face was all scrunched up and red. "You're a real bitch. I mean, the first night you came to Wine Down Wednesday the ladies were like, 'Oh, Bella is so nice, she's so pretty, blah, blah, blah.' I didn't get it. You're not that special. You're nothing but a troublemaker."

"You know what? You can call me all the names in the book and blame me for your shitty little life. I'm all out of fucks to give. If I were you, I'd take a good hard look in the mirror and realize, you're the problem."

"All I did was get cheated on by my husband and take the only comfort that was offered to me. Do you have any idea how horrible it is to have your life blown-up twice? I was a good wife to my ex, and I was giving Lance something he wasn't getting at home. You better pray to God nothing like this ever happens to you. You and your perfect husband that no one has ever met. What does anyone in this neighborhood really know about you? You pass judgment and play hero and pretend to be this great friend, but no one knows you. Who are you, Bella Wright?"

This conversation was going in circles. I should've never engaged with Julie, who was incapable of accepting responsibility for her actions. Catherine was right. She was a narcissist. A textbook case of narcissism.

Without a word, I walked away as Julie continued to hurl insults in my direction. Then it hit me as I rounded the bend and found my way home. Every husband was cheating on his wife, except for one, Dave. And my gut told me Dave was capable of murder.

CHAPTER FORTY-SIX

AFTER I GOT SHOWERED AND dressed for the day, my anxiety was in overdrive, so I set up a mini workstation in my kitchen.

Sleuthing 101 took my mind off of my run-in with Julie. A few hours later, I'd connected more dots on the cold case from my old neighborhood. Even though my kitchen was a disaster, I was almost there.

After I pried open the junk drawer and emptied out some of the stuff to make room for my secret folder of newspaper clippings, a knock on the door jolted me. Maybe I shouldn't answer. Lately, no good news was waiting on the other side of the door.

When the knocking persisted, I gave up and greeted the person standing on my front stoop. This was a welcome sight.

"Hey, Abby. How are you?" I asked in a cheerful tone.

"I'm… okay. Could I come in and talk to you for a second?"

"Sure. I need to take a break anyhow."

We both settled in on the sofa. "What brings you by?"

Abby cleared her throat. "Well… it's about my brother-in-law, Jeremy. Vanessa mentioned you two crossed paths at the bookstore, and he was kind of abrupt. I wanted to apologize."

"Oh, there's no need. I felt a little awkward, you know, like I was in the way. But it's private. You don't owe me an explanation."

"Thanks… I appreciate that."

Abby's body language was difficult to read, did she want to tell me more?

"Um… if… you feel like talking though," I said and braced myself for more secrets.

"I don't want to bother you with my stuff. I mean, sometimes I wonder if I've burdened my friends so much that I should go to a therapist."

"There's no shame in that. I've done therapy."

"Hmm… yeah… that's probably what I should do," Abby replied and stared out my front window. "You know, this neighborhood is so beautiful. Did you notice when the leaves fell, they looked like some sort of perfect autumn photo on Pinterest? I've never lived anywhere this nice, and yet, I'd live in a van if it meant things could go back to the way they were."

Houston, she has a problem…

"Listen, Abby, if you need to vent or get something off your chest, I'm a pretty good listener."

"You honestly wouldn't mind?"

"Not at all. I'm sorry you're going through something. Has your boyfriend been helping you?"

"Well… Ethan, my perfect boyfriend, thinks I'm overreacting, and that I should cut my sister, Amy, some slack. So does Jeremy, her husband. Now I'm questioning myself."

"I'm afraid I don't know all the ins and outs of the situation, but if your sister did something unforgivable, maybe you need more time apart."

"My sister did something criminal and it almost got me killed."

"Woah. It sounds like an episode of one of my true crime podcasts."

"Yeah, I mean, do we really know anyone, or what goes on behind closed doors?"

"I've discovered the answer is no. Maybe time can't heal this wound."

"I'm not sure anything can help. The problem is she had an undiagnosed mental illness. My brother-in-law says Amy suffered a psychotic break after the last failed attempt at IVF. You know how you hear about mothers with postpartum depression doing horrible things, like drowning their own children? It's sort of like that, only for Amy it was more of a slippery, gradual slope. That's how it was explained to me. And there was also a lot of built-up resentment toward me about things from our childhood. She suffered terrible, unspeakable horror in order to keep me safe."

"Wow, I don't know what to say. Is she getting help?"

"Yes, for now. She pleaded guilty to a lesser charge, hoping she wouldn't do jail time. She's been in a psychiatric facility until she is sentenced next month. Jeremy wants me to speak to the judge on her behalf. I've been dragging my feet and haven't made a decision. This all happened back in early September. I mean, that's when I found out about everything."

"So, it's still fresh. You must be traumatized."

"I am. It's one of the reasons I stay home most of the time. I get anxious. Ethan, he's a little more social. There's a bar he loves called Tom and Tony's and I haven't been able to go there since… well… for a long time. I go to the bookstore because Turn the Page is my happy place. I feel peaceful when I'm in there, but now that I know Jeremy went there looking for me, I'm sure I'll avoid that too."

"What's holding you back from putting a good word in for your sister? I totally get where you're coming from, but maybe going to prison isn't the best thing for her."

"That's what Ethan and Jeremy say. I guess for me, this huge fracture between us feels like a death. My parents weren't around much. All I had was my big sister, Amy. Now I've lost her too, but the weird thing is, I don't think I ever had her to begin with. She was really good at pretending and making me think it was us against the world. I never knew the real Amy. Her husband didn't either, but I think Jeremy is holding on too tightly to someone who didn't exist. He blames himself. He said he missed all the signs and dove headfirst into his new job in Hope Ridge. He remembers telling her that he wanted to quit trying to get pregnant after the last round of IVF didn't work and there was a shift, a change in her personality, but he thought it would pass."

"I would imagine the hormones alone could have an effect."

"Yeah. But in Amy's case, I think it goes deeper than that. You know, sometimes I think we all talk too much and don't listen nearly enough. Maybe she realized at an early age that no one was listening or cared. I used to feel like that, but I had her. She didn't have anyone. Maybe that's why she started putting on her fake facade and told people what they wanted to hear. Oh, God! Now I'm the one doing all the talking and not allowing you to say anything. They didn't call me Gabby Abby in school for nothing."

I chuckled. "For what it's worth, I like Gabby Abby very much. Out of all the women I've met in the neighborhood, you seem the most honest. You aren't faking anything."

"No. Even if I wasn't a chatterbox, my face gives me away every time."

"That's because you can move your face. Everyone else has too much Botox."

She busted out laughing. "Oh, God. You noticed that too?"

"One-hundred percent. My goodness, forgive me. I haven't even offered you anything. Would you like a cup of tea or some sparkling water or something?"

"Tea sounds great."

"Perfect. You sit tight and I'll be right back."

I hopped off the sofa and headed into my kitchen. Good Lord! I didn't realize what a mess I'd made. In a panic, I gathered up the rest of the papers strewn everywhere when Abby appeared in the archway.

Her expression turned grim as she surveyed the state of things. "You know... um... I'm going to need to take a raincheck on the tea. I just remembered something I had to do."

"Oh... that's a shame. Uh... sorry about this mess. I got a little carried away working on something."

Her gaze traveled to the raspberry jelly smeared on the counter and the open peanut butter jar with the knife sticking out. "No worries. Happens to me all the time. So... you know... I'll see you around. And... have a great Thanksgiving. Can you believe it's this Thursday?"

"No, I really can't."

Abby did a quick about-face and headed to the door. "I hope you have a good one."

Flushed with embarrassment, I took off my hoodie and followed her. "Yeah, you too. Before you leave, I wanted to ask you about Hope Ridge Publishing. Vanessa said you didn't need any proofreaders right now, but if something opens up, please keep me in mind."

"Yeah, sure." Abby glanced at my shirt and asked with a tremble in her voice. "Are you okay? Is your husband coming home soon or... maybe someone is coming over?"

I stared right into her eyes wondering why they were filled with fear. "It's been a rough day. Actually, a rough couple of weeks. I was hoping that maybe I could finally tell someone what was going on with me."

She sucked in a breath. "Yeah. Of course. Um... I just forgot about something I have to do. Next time. I'll stop by after Thanksgiving."

With that, she rushed out the door as if my house was on fire. Once she was gone, I traipsed back to the kitchen and caught a glimpse of my reflection in the toaster. My T-shirt had a red stain on it. Was it from the jelly? Did that freak Abby out?

"Well, I guess she scares easily," I muttered to myself as I pulled the knife out of the peanut butter and licked it clean.

Next time — that was what all the women said — I would love to hear about you next time. No one knew my secrets. Just as well. They couldn't handle the truth.

CHAPTER FORTY-SEVEN

"Hey, Bella, it's me," Catherine said late Tuesday afternoon over the phone. "Did you get my text last night?"

After Abby left my house, I put my phone on silent and went back to playing detective. I worked all night until I cracked the case.

"No, I'm sorry," I replied. "Something came up. I'm glad you called though. I've been worried about you."

"Don't be. I'm a whole new woman. I'm officially separated from Mick the lying Dick. I'm taking my life back."

"Good for you. In my own way, I am too. Hard work pays off."

"That's wonderful. And… of course, I want to hear all about it as soon as I get back from my trip."

"Where are you going?"

"Last minute trip. I'm flying out tomorrow to visit my daughter. I'll be back after the holidays. That's why I texted you. I was wondering if you had an extra set of luggage I could borrow. When Mick packed his bags, he took my best Louis Vuitton suitcase, and since I'm going to be gone for six weeks. I could use a couple of extra bags. I don't have time to shop, I need to start packing ASAP."

"Oh… yeah. I think there are a couple of extra ones I don't use anymore. You're welcome to them. I don't think I'm going anywhere anytime soon."

Catherine squealed, "You're a doll. Thank you. Just pop by when you get a free minute. My plane leaves first thing in the morning, and I'm running like a chicken with his head cut off, which is better than

Mick. I caught him so flat-footed, he's scrambling like two cheating, rotten eggs fighting in a frying pan."

I chuckled. "Good for you. I'm just going to pop in the shower, and I'll bring them by. And if you have a second, maybe I could talk while you pack. There's something I need to tell you. It's important."

"Uh… sure… sure, if there's time. I have to run for now. Bye."

When I got upstairs, I found the extra suitcases in one of the spare bedrooms and hauled them downstairs. After I fetched a bottle of water, I went back upstairs for a shower.

While I toweled off, I wiped the fog off of the mirror and stared at myself. In this bright light, I looked haggard. Had I lost weight? My cheeks were sunken in and the bags under my eyes were more pronounced than ever.

Was that why Abby asked me if I was okay? One thing was for sure. Everyone talked and no one listened. It was a real shame. I had a lot to say.

CHAPTER FORTY-EIGHT

"BELLA, HI! COME ON IN," Catherine said as she grabbed the suitcases from me and left them in her foyer. "Did you carry these all the way from your house?"

"Yeah. They aren't that heavy," I replied and blew on my cold hands. "I should've worn my husband's gloves though. It's freezing. They're calling for snow tomorrow and Thursday."

"Oh, bite your tongue. No one wants a white Thanksgiving. It will make the airlines a mess."

"That's true. So… there's something I've been wanting to tell you."

Catherine cut me off, "Hold that thought. I have someone I want you to meet."

"Really? You know, I didn't slap on any makeup. I probably look a mess. I'll leave you to your guest and we can chat another time."

She clasped me by the elbow. "Nonsense. You're fine. It's my lawyer. You'll love her."

I'd love a lawyer? Doubtful, but I followed Catherine to her back room anyway. When we arrived, a put-together, beautiful blonde in an expensive, grey suit stood to greet me.

"Hi. You must be Bella. Catherine mentioned you were stopping by."

"Yeah, I brought her some extra luggage," I said "Nice to meet you."

"You too," she responded with a smile. "I'm Leigh, Catherine's lawyer. I'm helping her stick it to Mick."

Leigh? Was this Leigh Patterson, the woman who was supposed to go out with my brother, Anthony? I had to get out of here!

An uncomfortable laugh escaped. "Well, don't let me keep you from it. Have a safe trip, Catherine... and I'll... I'll see you next year."

Catherine waved her hand in the air. "Don't be silly. Stay for a second. Leigh was just telling me about a date she went on last week. He sounds like a keeper."

My stomach sank and panic filled my bones. "I... I should go."

"Bella, if I'm going to be gone over the holidays, you should get to know Leigh a little bit," Catherine insisted. "You need at least one other friend in the neighborhood that isn't part of our Wine Down Wednesday crowd. Not that we'll ever get those ladies together again. I was just filling Leigh in on the last one. What a nightmare, am I right?"

"So... you live in The Heights too?" I asked Leigh.

Leigh sat back down on the sofa. "Yes, I love it here. Actually, it's funny, the guy I went out with, Anthony, said his sister lives in The Heights as well."

"Small world," I mumbled.

Catherine clapped her hands together. "Bella, don't you have a brother named Anthony? Wouldn't it be crazy if it was the same guy?"

"The guy I went out with lives in Gettysburg. Where does your brother live?"

I cleared my throat while little beads of sweat broke out on my back. "Um... he lives in Gettysburg too."

Leigh scrunched up her face. "That's so weird. But obviously, it's not you because he told me his sister's name was Anna."

"Well, isn't Bella short for Annabelle?" Catherine replied.

I nodded. "Mmm... anyway, if you went out with my brother, I hope you had a great time. I've really got to go."

As I rushed to the door, Catherine was hot on my heels. "Bella, wait. What's wrong?"

"Nothing. My stomach has been acting up and you're busy, so I'm going home."

She stared at me as if she was trying to read my mind. "I feel like something is going on. I know I've been preoccupied with myself because of Mick, but if you need me…. I'm here. Are you sick? Is that it? You don't look well."

I thought I was ready to confide in someone. I had secrets too, but my gut told me not to. Instead, I spilled the beans on Nicole. "Uh… I've been keeping something from you."

"I knew it."

"Yeah, you're too smart for me. This situation between Dave and Nicole. It's weighing on me."

"What are you talking about? What situation?"

"Please don't say anything, but Dave has been abusive to Nicole. Her sprained wrist wasn't because she fell down the stairs."

Catherine gasped. "Oh, God. How do you know that?"

"She told me herself. Remember when she went to Pittsburgh? She wanted to move there with the girls, I mean, that was the plan until Dave found out about it. I have no idea what's going to happen with your real estate business, but get rid of Dave if you can. And please don't tell anyone anything. Dave is dangerous. I've had a few run-ins with him myself. If anything were to ever happen to Nicole, I'd never forgive myself for not saying something."

She wrapped her arms around me in an embrace. "Oh, you poor thing. No wonder you don't seem like yourself. What an awful burden for you to carry alone. Do you think she told Wendy and Julie?"

I broke our hug. "No, I don't think so. I saw Wendy and she said something about Nicole's arm being in a sling and that she fell into the wall on her way to the bathroom. So, it seems like you and I are the only ones that know except for Nicole's mother. Nicole called me and begged me to keep quiet. She claimed Dave has turned over a new leaf and got the girls a cat, but I think it's only a matter of time before he does something else to her. I can't sleep because I keep imagining the worst."

Catherine's hand flew to her mouth. "Good God, I pray that doesn't happen. He's never shown one ounce of temper at the office. Dave is very mild-mannered. This is so difficult to wrap my head around."

"I know. I guess everyone has secrets. How much do we really know anyone?"

"And here I thought you were upset because Leigh went out on a date with your brother. That must be the farthest thing from your mind."

"Yeah… of course it is. Anyway, I'm going to go. Thanks for listening. I'm sorry to dump this on you and run, but I need to get home."

"Sure thing, hon. I'm only a phone call away if you need me. Don't hesitate to call or text."

"I won't. Be safe and have a wonderful time with your daughter."

We exchanged our good tidings of great joy for the holidays, and I raced home as fast as I could.

Once inside, I hurried upstairs and packed a bag of my own, as questions bombarded my mind. What did my brother say about me to Leigh? What would Leigh pass along to Catherine? Was it time to leave this neighborhood?

I was so close to finishing what I started when I came to Hope Ridge. Could the truth, my truth, be kept hidden for one more day? That was all I needed. Twenty-four hours before I vanished, again.

CHAPTER FORTY-NINE

MY PHONE WAS QUIET, TOO quiet. Was this the calm before the storm? I packed and cleaned and packed some more. I was so close to the end of my quest. All the puzzle pieces were in place. I cracked a five-year-old cold case from my former neighborhood and justice was in the palm of my hand.

When I relaxed on the bed and closed my eyes, I wondered if meeting Leigh today would blow up in my face. I'd been home for hours and I hadn't heard from Anthony... yet. Maybe he didn't bring me up on his first date. Surely, they had better topics to discuss than me, right?

Just as I was drifting off to sleep, my cell rang, and I jolted upright. Relief swept over me when I saw it was Jack, FaceTiming me. He almost never did that.

I answered right away, "Hi. Is something wrong?"

His warm smile greeted me. "No. Can't a husband want to see his wife without there being anything wrong? I miss you."

"I miss you too. You just never FaceTime, so I got worried."

"Well, there is something I want to talk to you about and I didn't think it could wait until tomorrow night."

Oh, boy, here it comes! "What is it? Please tell me you're not working on Thanksgiving."

"Of course not. I think the holiday is what gave me this epiphany. Honey, I can't stand being away from you four or five days a week. This isn't working anymore, and I was wondering if you would consider getting a townhouse closer to the city."

Tears filled my eyes. "Oh, Jack, are you serious? I would love that. I mean, at first, I thought this plan would work perfectly, but I hate being away from you too."

"I'm so relieved to hear you say that. I know you love the house and the neighborhood."

"I don't love anything more than I love you. You're the most important thing to me. We must be on the same wavelength. I've been packing and cleaning, hoping to get the hell out of here."

"You mean you'd really consider coming here for Thanksgiving?"

"Yeah. Remember that cold case from our old neighborhood I was working on? I finally cracked it. So, tomorrow after I take care of something, I'll get in the car and come to you."

Jack's expression changed and not for the better. "I thought we agreed to leave the past in the past."

"I never agreed to that. I need to right a wrong. Don't worry about a thing. I have a plan. And don't try to distract me with sex. It won't work this time."

He shook his head. "You have me at a disadvantage since I'm not there in person. What am I going to do over FaceTime? Whip out my dick?"

"It wouldn't be the first time," I said in a teasing tone, hoping to get him to laugh.

It worked. He chuckled. "Now who's distracting who? By the way, what are you wearing?"

I slid the phone down the length of my body. "As you can see, I'm very sexy, Mister Wright. This evening I'm featuring a lovely pair of sweatpants and a matching hoodie. I stole them from your winter collection. It got cold here."

"How do you make my old sweats look adorable? You have a gift, Mrs. Wright."

I held the cell steady, so he could see my face. "Hey, do you remember when you were on that first job right after we got married and we were sexting?"

"How could I forget? One-handed texting proved to be difficult, but worth it."

"Maybe for you. Remember, I tried to send you a photo of a certain area and I fell down. I just couldn't bend that way. My balance is terrible."

He cracked up so hard his phone shook. "My poor wifey. I was busy wanking it and you were picking yourself up off the floor."

"It was pretty funny. By the way, what are you wearing?"

Jack rose and gave me a full-length view of his grey sweats and black, long-sleeved T-shirt. Before he was done with his little show, he pulled his sweats down to give me a peek at the good stuff. "Do you like what you see?"

"You know I do. Is the striptease over? I thought you were going to take it off."

"Hey, I got to save something for when you get here tomorrow. I'm so glad you're coming, baby. It'll be a busy morning, but text me when you get on the road."

"I will. It'll depend on how soon I can wrap things up here. I'm anxious to put this long-awaited chapter behind me, behind us."

"You know you don't have to. You can just leave first thing in the morning and forget about it. Promise me you'll be careful."

"Of course. I love you, Jack."

"I love you too, baby. Night."

After I ended the call, I snuggled under the covers and thought, I would definitely be careful, but it wasn't me Jack should be worried about.

CHAPTER FIFTY

SHIT, SHIT, SHIT!

I overslept! In the middle of the night, I got up to use the bathroom and must've turned off my cell. My alarm was set for seven a.m. on my phone. It was after nine.

As I powered up my phone, I stumbled downstairs for coffee. Was my cell going to blow up? If I had messages from Anthony or Catherine, the answer was, yes.

Before I could find out, someone banging on the front door startled me.

"Anna! Anna, open the door or I'll break it down!"

Oh, no! Anthony. He knew. He knew everything.

With my heart racing, I rushed to open the door. "Anthony, what are you doing here?"

He barreled past me. "You know damn well why I'm here. God damn it, Anna. You promised me. You promised me you were done with this crap, and you were okay. You said you had moved on."

I shut the door, faced him in the hallway, and sucked in a breath. "I don't know what you're talking about. I'm totally fine. Do you want some coffee?"

"Jesus Christ. How can you sound so calm? I talked to Leigh this morning. She told me she met you last night. And after you left your friend's house, Catherine told Leigh about how your husband works in DC during the week. Leigh was concerned because when we went out, I told her the truth."

Dread filled every cell in my body as my voice quaked. "But…I'm not really lying."

Anthony grabbed me by the shoulders. "This has to stop! You have to let it go. Stop doing this to yourself."

"I... I... can't. It's real to me."

He glanced at the stairs, pushed me aside, and raced to the second floor. I followed behind him. "Anthony, wait! Don't go up there!"

In a rage, he threw open door after door, until he got to the primary bedroom. When he saw it, it stopped him dead in his tracks. "This is even worse than I thought."

His presence in this sacred space made me realize how insane it looked. "I'm sorry. I know you're disappointed in me."

"Sis, I'm not disappointed. I'm scared for you," he said in a softer tone. "This isn't normal."

"It's normal to me," I muttered.

Anthony picked up the navy blazer on the bed. "You said you got rid of this," he yelled and continued gathering pieces of Jack's clothes. "And you were supposed to throw this away and this and that."

I ripped Jack's things out of his hands and clutched them to my chest. "Stop! Don't touch them! They're mine. I mean, they're his."

"Jack's not... here, please tell me you know that."

Tears flooded my eyes. "No... no... don't say that. I feel like... he's still with me."

With gentle motions, Anthony took Jack's clothes out of my arms and put them back on the bed. "You have to let him go."

When he headed for the door, I asked, "Where are you going?"

"I'm going downstairs to get a garbage bag and throw all of his stuff away."

"Don't do that, please. I'll get rid of it. I promise."

"Anna, you've made me a lot of promises and you haven't kept any of them. This isn't healthy. You've left me no choice."

"But... it's all I have. Please, I'm begging you."

"Look, I get it. Jack… he… he left and then Mom and Dad passed away right after that. Your world was shattered, mine too. But… it's been five years. Five years and time in and out of the hospital. I know you don't want to go back to the psych ward at Brookhaven. Do you?"

"No. I hated it there. It was scary as hell. They didn't help me. All they did was drug me."

"Then pack a bag and come to my house. This neighborhood was a terrible idea. I should've never allowed you to move here. You weren't ready."

"I can't go with you, not yet. There's something I need to do here first."

"What? You better tell me right now."

"It's private. I can't tell anyone."

"That's not going to fly. There's no way in hell I'm leaving you alone again."

"Why not? Everyone leaves. Jack left me, your wife left you, what difference does it make?"

"It's not the same thing and you know it."

"I'll tell you what I know. Five years ago, I was happy. Was life perfect? No, but it was pretty damn great. Jack and I had a beautiful house in the suburbs of Pittsburgh, remember?"

"Of course, I remember."

"You, your ex, Danny, Mom and Dad would all come for Thanksgiving. I mean, Brenda, the ex, was a bitch, but we'd ply her with wine and plop her down in front of the TV so we could have our time together. I was living my dream and I don't think I fully took those precious moments in. That's why I'm trying so hard to hang on. In a flash, everything can be taken away."

"I know how you feel, but we have to move on with our lives. You can start over. You're only forty-seven."

"I'm not forty-seven. I'm forty-two."

His pained expression puzzled me. "No. Anna, you're forty-seven years old. I'm in my fifties. Oh, God... I don't know what to do."

Was I forty-seven? I held my head in my hands as my brain raged. "You don't have to do anything. I'm fine. I swear I'm fine."

"How can you say that? You're so buried in the past, you don't even know how old you are?"

I cleared my throat. "It was a slip of the tongue. We were talking about the past, so I was thinking about when I was forty-two. It was the last year I was happy. I had Jack, Mom, and Dad. I had a life. When Jack... left, it felt like time stood still. I'm okay, Anthony. You don't need to babysit me. Remember when you came here for soup? I seemed good, right?"

"That's because I didn't come upstairs and see all of Jack's stuff that you said you got rid of. I knew something was off when I saw you set your dining room table for two, but I let it go, and now you have to let Jack go once and for all."

"Anthony, I can't. He's still a part of my life. I see him. It's like we're still together."

With a sigh, he flopped on the bed. "But you're not."

"Look, why don't you forget about what Catherine told Leigh and do what you were going to do today? I kind of have a lot going on too. We'll talk more tomorrow."

"And if I leave, you'll be okay?"

"Of course," I replied and saw his shoulders relax.

Anthony had to go. I couldn't allow him to interfere in my plans. I'd waited too long for this day. As he rose from the bed, victory washed over me. He was going. I was sure of it.

"Let me walk you out," I said.

232

Last night's phone conversation with Jack danced in my mind. I'd be with him again soon. He wanted me to come to DC.

In a few hours, I would take care of business here, pack up my car, and leave this neighborhood behind. I wouldn't make the mistake again of being everyone's sounding board and doing all the listening while everyone else did the talking. I would disappear and rewrite my story. Jack would be proud of me for righting a wrong. With everything in me, I knew that much was true.

Lost in my Jack daydream, I almost didn't hear Anthony when he headed to our bedroom door. "So… Thanksgiving… Anna? Anna, what the hell?"

"I'm sorry what were you saying?"

"Tomorrow is Thanksgiving. I'll come by and pick you up. You can come and eat with Danny and me."

I smiled, thinking about Jack. "Oh, I'm sorry. I already have plans. Jack wants me to join him in DC. I'll see Danny another time. Would that be okay?"

In an instant, he was in my face, fuming. "What the fuck are you talking about? Jack is dead!"

CHAPTER FIFTY-ONE

"YOU TAKE THAT BACK!" I screamed and slapped Anthony across the face. "Fuck you for saying that."

He grasped me by my wrists. "Stop it! Stop this shit right now. I won't take it back. It's the goddamn truth. Your husband is dead. He died of a heart attack while he was jogging five years ago."

I wriggled and fought to break his hold on me while tears streamed down my face. "No! No! No! He's not gone. I see him! Stop saying he's dead. He's with me. It's true. It's real."

"Then where are they? Tell me!"

"Where's what? I don't know what you're talking about."

Anthony tossed me on the bed and hurried to the bathroom sink. "I know you're taking something."

As he rifled through the medicine cabinet and drawers, I yelled, "Stop! That's not true. I'm not taking anything."

He stilled and turned to me with a baggy in his hand. "Then what is this shit, huh? What are they? Some kind of magic mushrooms. You swore to me you wouldn't even drink alcohol anymore?"

"I'm not drinking," I said with my voice trembling.

"Where did you get this?"

"I don't remember," I sobbed, "but I take them on the weekends and Jack comes back to me. I know you want me to let him go, but I can't. I can't do it."

Anthony tossed the sack on the sink and came to me as I wailed. "I know it's hard. I miss him too. Sometimes I find myself talking to him, just like Mom and Dad."

"It's not fair. He should still be here."

"I agree. But his dad passed young of a heart attack too, remember?"

I wiped my tears. "Jack didn't die of a heart attack. He was healthy. He was a runner. Jack was killed. I know it."

"Sis, you've got to stop. The autopsy said heart attack."

"But what about the damage to the right side of his body? When Jack went for a jog, he ran against the traffic. If he had a heart attack, wouldn't he have fallen on his left side or back, or on his face? Someone did something. Someone hit him and took off. He had a heart attack because he was struck by a car. I feel that in my bones."

He sat on the bed next to me. "I know you've always expected foul play, but the truth is, it doesn't matter. It's not going to bring him back."

"But don't you get it? I can't move on until the person who is responsible pays for what they did. If you thought someone killed Danny, wouldn't you move heaven and earth to find out who did it?"

"I guess. But… they closed Jack's case. They said it was a heart attack."

"You know there were six families that moved out of my neighborhood after Jack died. I've been tracking them for the last five years. I still have screenshots of their social media posts from the night Jack was killed, so I could see who had an alibi and who didn't. I think someone knows something or saw something."

"You're not a detective, how are you doing this?"

"It's my little hobby you find so unsettling, my true crime blogs. I've become sort of a quiet, savvy sleuth. I was able to eliminate a few of the families right away, and with patience and a lot of work, I'm pretty sure I know who hit Jack."

"Then go to the police. If this is what's going to give you closure, that's fine, but you can't take the law into your own hands. I don't think Jack would want you to do that."

"How do you know what Jack wants? You've moved on from everything so easily. I didn't even see you cry when Mom and Dad died."

"Are you kidding? There were tears, but I had to stay strong for you. I kept thinking if I fell apart who would hold you together."

"Your strength made me feel... weak and crazy, which I guess I am. The thing is, I knew I couldn't come here and be Anna, the sad widow with the long, dark hair. No one wanted to be around her. I thought I had friends, but I was wrong. People stayed away from me. They acted like tragedy and grief were contagious. So, I became Bella, the married woman who has this amazing husband that comes home on weekends. I'm telling you, Anthony, sometimes I don't even need to take anything for Jack to be real to me."

"But he isn't real. Please tell me you know that."

"Of course I do. That's why I don't take those mushrooms all the time. I have to keep a level head so I can get information. I can't let anyone know the real me, so I hide behind a persona. It's been like a chess game or a part in a play, and pretty soon the show will be over. I found a therapist here, Doctor Heather Perrot. I'll get myself well again. I just need to finish this first."

He exhaled. "I'm sorry. I can't let you do that. I need you to come with me."

I talked over him. "Did you know that Jack and I had a fight the night he went out for that jog? It was so stupid. Jack kept leaving the empty milk container in the fridge. I mentioned it to him several times. He worked late that day. I made dinner, but we never ate it. Instead, he came home when I was in the shower and poured himself a dish of cereal, honey nut Cheerios. When I came downstairs, I thought cereal sounded like a good idea and when I got the milk out of the fridge, the container was empty, again. And... I lost it. I started pissing and moaning about how inconsiderate he was, how he didn't even call to tell me he was going to be late, we never ate dinner together, and on and on. I must've sounded like a Howler monkey. I just kept bitching at him. He never said a word. He sat down the half-eaten bowl of cereal, put on his tennis shoes, and took off."

"You never told me that before."

My voice quivered and a lump formed in my throat. "I never told anyone. The last words he heard me say to him were so awful and mean. If I had only shut the hell up, he would still be here. He wouldn't have gone for that run to get away from me. I hate myself for that. I'll hate myself until the day I die. It's eaten me alive for five years."

"Jack would run late at night all the time. This isn't your fault. Don't do this to yourself. You've been through enough."

"To this day, I can't eat cereal. I can't even go down the aisle in the grocery store, and I never buy milk either. The only thing that got me through was hunting down the person who hit him. I'm about ninety-nine percent sure who did it and once they've been dealt with, I will move on. I'll accept that Jack's dead. I'll start over. You know, sometimes when I see him in a dream or a hallucination, we still fight, only now I back down. Sometimes, when I'm dreaming, he goes for a run, and I freak out. I can't stop him. Why didn't I stop him that night?"

"None of this is your fault. The losses you suffered in such a short time would take a toll on anyone. Jack was your person. He was a damn good guy."

I knew my brother too well and what he was about to say before he said it. In order to finish what I started

I would have to play a little chess game right now and be strategic. And lie if I had to.

With an exhale, he hauled himself off the bed. "I'm glad we talked, and I think it's best if you packed a bag and came with me."

"Yeah, I guess you're probably right."

"You're not going to fight me?"

"No, I heard what you said, and I agree. I shouldn't take the law into my own hands. I have to let this go. Saying all of this out loud has done me a world of good. I feel so much better."

"Are you serious? You're not screwing with me?"

"Of course not. Anthony, you know me better than anyone. Look, if it'll make you feel better, throw those mushrooms away. I'm telling you, I'm done with all of it."

He went to the bathroom sink, took the baggie, and shoved them into the front pocket of his jeans while I winced on the inside.

"How long will it take you to pack?" he asked.

"I'll need at least an hour," I fibbed.

An alarm sounded and Anthony checked his cell. "Damn it."

"What's wrong?"

"I set a reminder to go pick up Danny from the airport. It's the day before Thanksgiving. I'm sure the traffic will be nuts."

"Then you should go. I'll be fine."

"Why don't you come with me, and we'll swing back here and have you pack up your stuff."

"I haven't even showered yet or had any coffee. It's going to take me some time. I want to stay with you for a while if that's okay. I need to cancel the mail and chuck everything in the fridge. You go. It will give me time to get organized."

He stared at me, contemplating his next move. "Yeah, okay. Promise me you won't do anything crazy?"

I cracked a wide grin. "You have my word, I won't do anything crazy."

With reluctance, Anthony left. After we said our goodbyes, I stood at the big bay window and gave him a thumbs-up.

Once his car pulled away, I mumbled to myself, "Sorry, brother dear, promises were made to be broken."

CHAPTER FIFTY-TWO

IT ALL CAME DOWN TO the next two hours. My plotting, planning, and detective work was about to come to fruition. Jack's death would not be in vain. Someone was going to pay.

With my careful, nosy neighbor skills, I turned up on the culprit's doorstep at precisely the right moment.

Get in and get out. Don't waste time getting emotional. You have a job to do.

When their front door opened, they didn't appear happy to see me.

"Bella, what on earth are you doing here?"

"Are you alone?"

"Yes, Dave ran a quick errand. Come in before you freeze to death," Nicole said.

Nicole Taylor from Mount Lebanon, just outside of Pittsburgh. I've been looking for you, you heartless piece of shit.

"Thanks," I said and stepped into their foyer. "Where are the girls?"

"They went shopping. Of course, they waited until the last minute to get me a birthday gift."

"And Dave is with them?"

"No, I sent him to Paul's Market for pies. You know, pumpkin and apple. The usual Thanksgiving stuff. He forgot about dessert when he put in his order at Fat Russell's."

"Oh… and where's Paul's Market? I haven't been there."

"The opposite end of town toward Greencastle."

"So… how are things going with you and Dave?"

"Great! Never better. But my mom keeps saying it won't last. You know that he's love bombing me. I had to hide my burner phone in my closet because she doesn't let up."

"She's probably just worried about you. I am too. I don't want to get you in trouble by being here. I know he doesn't care for me."

"It's okay. Dave should be back in about a half hour. Lord knows when Emily and Sarah will come back. I gave them my credit card, so they're probably shopping for themselves too."

"Well, I won't keep you. I just feel bad. I ordered you something from Amazon for your birthday and it won't get here until Friday."

My body was relaxed and peaceful while I lied my ass off. I was sure Nicole had no idea that I came to kill her. All I needed to do was remain calm, friendly, get information, and make her admit what she did.

Let's play chess!

"You got me a birthday present?" Nicole asked with excitement in her voice.

"Of course. You've become such a wonderful friend. I really appreciate you."

"I appreciate you too, Bella. I mean that. You were there for me when I needed someone. Do you want a glass of wine or something? Take off your coat and gloves and stay a while. Dave will text me when he's almost home."

"I'm good. I'm still so cold from the walk over here. You know what I would love, um… I would love to meet your cat. I was thinking about getting one myself."

"Oh! I think you should. We adore our little Ambrose. He's downstairs on the lower level where the girls spend most of their time. Come on. I'll take you to our furry kid."

I followed behind her on our way to the lower level, which was an extra fancy way of saying basement. While this was the nicest "lower level" I'd seen, it was still a basement and smelled like stale, musty, flowers.

"Ambrose," Nicole called from the middle of the TV area. "Here, little buddy. He's probably hiding in Emily's room. It's messier than Sarah's, more fun, I guess."

"You know, I used to have a cat, but it was killed. Someone hit him with a car and drove off. Can you believe that?"

Her upper lip twitched. "That's horrible. Who would do that?"

"Right? What kind of person hits something or someone, and just keeps going? I mean, what kind of world are we living in?"

"You're so right, Bella."

"You know what? I should apologize to you. I haven't been totally honest. Bella isn't short for Annabelle. I made that up. I guess being in a new neighborhood, I wanted a fresh start. I suppose a lot of people do that, change their name, dye their hair a different color. And while I'm being honest, my last name isn't Wright. My husband and I used to call each other Mister and Mrs. Right. It was our pet name for each other."

"What uh... what is your last name?"

"Williams. And even though everyone called my husband Jack, his given name was Jonathon. Jonathon Williams. Ring any bells?"

"I–I–I'm not sure," she stuttered.

"Let me break it down for you. You and I are from the same neighborhood, outside of Pittsburgh, Mount Lebanon. I've never lived in Chicago. I lied, just like you did. I've been looking for you for five years, and I think you know why."

All the color drained from her face and her voice quaked. "I... I don't know what you're talking about."

I cocked my head, taking a few steps toward her. "Oh, but I think you do. The hunter-green sedan covered in your garage was one of the first clues that told me I had finally found the family I'd been searching for. I suppose it's time for a few confessions. I put Visine eye drops in an open bottle of red wine the first time I came to your house, so your daughters would get ill if they drank it. That way I could come and check on them the next day. You know, get in good with the head bitch in charge of the neighborhood. I also made up the profile, Colin Smith, on Instagram to stalk Emily in the hopes you would come to me for help. You fell right into my trap. Since your husband seemed suspicious of me, I threw him off the scent with the flowers I accidentally on purpose sent to your house. A pretty genius move, wouldn't you say? And I brought ice to your house on that first Wine Down Wednesday so I would have a chance to look in your garage and see if you were hiding anything. *Oof!* So much damage to the front end on the passenger side of the car you covered up. I guess my husband really screwed it up when you hit him and left him for dead! Admit it. Five years ago you hit Jonathon Williams, my Jack. You killed him."

She backed away. "No. No, I swear I didn't. It wasn't me."

I applauded her and laughed. "Wow! Thank you. I thought it would be tough to get you to crack. You just gave yourself away. You admit that you know what happened to my husband."

"No… God, I'm so confused. You told everyone your husband worked in DC and came home on the weekends, now you're in my basement telling me he's dead and you think I killed him?"

"Yes! Bravo! Now you're up to speed."

"So, what? What are you going to do about it? Go to the police? You don't have any real proof of anything."

"You're right. I'm sure they would look at all my clues, pat me on the head, and send the poor grieving widow on her way. That's why I'm here. To take the law into my own hands. To get justice. Did you know that right after Jack was killed, my parents died? That's a lot of grief piled on top of grief. It's enough to make someone snap."

She inched away from me until she ran into the armrest of the couch. "I'm so sorry that happened to you, but I had nothing to do with your husband. I mean, of course, I heard about a Jonathon Williams dying while he was jogging. It was all over the news and everyone in our neighborhood talked about it, but didn't he die of a heart attack?"

"A heart attack brought on by being struck by a car. The car that's in your garage. I have more proof than you think I do. It might be in your best interest to just admit it and tell me what happened that night."

While her eyes darted around the room, searching for a way out, I realized there was a tiny possibility she wasn't behind the wheel, but at this point, I couldn't allow her to live. She knew too much, and I didn't know enough — yet. I had to act fast and get out of here before Dave got home. With any luck, he'd be home before the girls, he'd find her lifeless body, call the police, and be taken into custody.

Nicole huffed and bluffed. She knew she'd been had. "I don't see why I should tell you anything. You're obviously crazy and planning to kill me. But I don't think you have the guts, so... why don't we make a deal. You turn around and leave, and I won't tell anyone you came into my house making threats."

"What do I get in return? See... this doesn't sound like the best deal for me."

"I'll keep my mouth shut about your nonexistent husband who doesn't work in DC."

"Yeah... that's not going to cut it. You're right about one thing. I am crazy, like, certifiable, and I do plan on killing you. Also, I will get away with it. Just answer me one question first, when you hit my husband with your car, was it an accident or did you do it on purpose?"

"No, I don't know," she yelled.

"When you drove away, did you know that you killed him?"

"I… I wasn't driving the car!" she shrieked. "I was drunk in the back seat!"

"What? You're lying!"

Tears streamed down her face. "I'm not! I wish I was! My God. That night has been haunting me. It ruined our lives."

I lunged for her and grabbed her by the throat. "It ruined your lives? What the fuck did you think it did to mine?"

"Let go of me."

"Only if you start talking."

"Okay!" She gasped and I backed away.

"I'll tell you everything," she panted. "I was at a friend's house, and we were drinking — a lot. Well, I was drinking too much. Dave had cracked me across the face the night before because I passed out on the couch and Sarah became so anxious, she threw up. Back then that was all he'd do, slap me. He was always on my case about how much alcohol I drank. The thing is, I drank because he started hitting me. Not all the time, but enough to make me want to numb myself. The girls came with me to the friend's house, and they hung out with their kids. When it was time to leave, I couldn't drive home, and there was no way I was calling Dave. Even if I wasn't afraid to call him, I knew I couldn't. He was getting an award at a work event. People were tagging him in photos on Facebook, so I thought I had time to get home and go to bed before he realized I was drunk. Since we weren't that far from the house, I let Emily drive. She'd just gotten her learner's permit. She's the one who hit your husband, but it was my fault. Emily had never driven at night. She didn't know where the lights were. Sarah was scared and kept yelling at Emily to turn the lights on. It happened so fast. When the girls screamed it sobered me up real quick. I saw his lifeless body on the curb, and I panicked. We took off. We left him there."

A growling sound ripped from my throat as I tackled her on the couch. She fought and cried out, but the fury that burned in my blood for the last five years helped me pin her down. I wrapped my gloved hand around her throat and squeezed while Nicole's helpless, hushed cries filled the air.

"Just give in," I spat. "I won't stop until you're dead. And when Dave finds you, he'll call 911 and he'll get arrested. I've already been to the police. They have the photos I took of your back. And of course all the text messages from your mom on your burner phone. The last thing I'll do before I leave here is make sure Dave's DNA is on these gloves. He'll be in jail for the rest of his life."

Little murmurs and squelching noises sounded from Nicole as her body was giving up. "That's it, Nicole. Let go, because I'm not going to."

When she tried to speak, I brought my face close to hers. "What is it? Any last words?"

With a whisper, she said, "You'll never get away with this."

I smiled, using two hands to squeeze the last breaths out of her body, and replied, "Of course, I will. Everybody knows when a wife turns up murdered, it's always the husband."

Dead…

CHAPTER FIFTY-THREE

Six months later

"GOOD MORNING, MRS. WILLIAMS. HOW did you sleep?" Becky, the sweet nurse on the early shift asked me.

"Excellent. You know, Becky, you can call me Anna. I see you almost every day. We don't need to be so formal."

She smiled wide. "Thank you, Anna. I appreciate it. Would you like your breakfast in your room today or will you be coming to the dining hall?"

"In my room is fine," I replied. "Can you add me to the noon yoga class if it isn't full?"

"Of course. I'll get your breakfast tray ready. Oh. And you have a visitor waiting. Shall I send him in?"

Him? It was probably my brother, Anthony. "Sure, that would be fine. I just need five minutes. Thanks so much."

After Becky left me on my own, I let out a contented sigh. It had been six months since I killed Nicole with my leather-gloved hands. Five months since I transferred myself to "Fresh Beginnings," a new-age mental health and wellness center in Virginia.

The first month I was placed on a thirty-day hold in the psych ward at the hospital. I attempted to un-alive myself the day after Thanksgiving. The hell I'd put Anthony through was selfish of me. I'd figured since I righted the wrong of Jack's death, I should go be with him. Now I realize that wasn't right. Even though I held no great affection for this earthly plane, it wasn't up to me to decide when I died. When it was my time, I would gladly go and be with Jack and my parents.

While I was still here, I worked on myself. For the first time in five years, I went through the stages of grief and healing. Fresh Beginnings was the perfect and extremely expensive place for me to be.

Thank you, Mom and Dad, for leaving me a small fortune in your will so I could afford to get healthy.

Little by little, I got stronger and faced the truth. My husband was gone. My parents were gone, but I had a brother that loved me.

And I got away with murder.

Dave was arrested, and in jail, awaiting trial for killing Nicole. My timing that day couldn't have been more ideal. The second she was dead, Dave texted her to say he was a few minutes away. I took off Jack's old leather gloves and hid them in Dave's hamper before I left their house. Then I went to my backyard and burned the thin rubber gloves I wore underneath.

With my bags already packed, I drove to Anthony's house in Gettysburg instead of waiting for him to pick me up. I left The Heights and never looked back.

I also blocked everyone from that toxic neighborhood. I would never speak to them again. Well, I never got to speak anyway, I was just a sounding board for them. The days of those self-involved women dumping their crap on me were over. Being a good listener was for chumps.

Doctor Heather Perrot was the only person from Hope Ridge that I'd kept in touch with. She had moved to Virginia, opened her own practice, and volunteered her time at Fresh Beginnings.

The one thing I couldn't talk to anyone about was my lack of guilt for killing Nicole. I didn't feel bad... I didn't feel anything when it came to her. Of course, my non-compassionate state troubled me, but I would have to take this secret to my grave.

My days consisted of yoga, Pilates, art class, and chess. I learned how to play chess, and even though I wasn't very good, I kept a board in my room. It was part of this facility's wellness plan. "A mind and body engaged is a mind that's healing."

I was healing. I could speak about Jack and his death freely. I was able to eat honey nut Cheerios again. Baby steps were still steps.

After I brushed my teeth and put on a clean yoga outfit, there was a knock on the door.

"Come in," I called and got the shock of my life when I saw him.

"Hello there, you're looking well."

What the hell was Lance, Wendy's husband, doing here?

"Oh, hi! How... uh... what are you doing here?" I asked.

"Delivering breakfast, for one thing," Lance said with a grin and placed my tray on the bedside table.

"Oh, thank you. I'm sorry, I'm a bit confused... are you here as my doctor?"

"Yes and no. I came to town to have lunch today with my former colleague, Doctor Perrot. She mentioned her volunteer work at this center and that she was seeing a patient from my old neighborhood. We've met before, do you remember?"

Of course, I remembered Doctor Lance Anderson. Who could forget the way he leered at me.

"I... uh... yeah... I remember," I replied. "Aren't my appointments with Doctor Perrot supposed to be confidential?"

His intense blue eyes gazed into mine. "Well, I guess it will be our little secret. You like secrets, don't you, Bella? Oh, that's right, your name isn't Bella, it's Anna, correct?"

My mouth went dry. "Yeah. I guess I wasn't completely honest when I moved into my house in The Heights."

"No worries. Anyway, I came to town a little early to have a look around this facility and check in on you.

Wendy misses you. She's been going through a rough time. You know... because of Nicole."

A knot formed in my stomach. "Uh... yeah. I heard about that. Such a shame."

Lance gestured to the breakfast tray. "Aren't you going to eat?"

I shrugged. "I'm not all that hungry. Maybe later."

His focus was drawn to my chess board. "You play chess?"

"A little. I'm not very good."

"I love chess. I've got some time before my lunch, how about a game?"

"Oh... you don't want to play with a novice like me. It would be boring."

"Nonsense," Lance said and with care placed the board on my bed. "Come, sit. I'll let you choose, black or white, and give you the opening move."

Lance wasn't going to take no for an answer. The only way to get him out of here was to let him beat me in as few moves as possible.

"I'll take black," I replied as we both sat on the bed.

"Sounds perfect. Your move."

In an effort to speed this game along, I deliberately exposed my king, paving the way to a quick defeat.

Lance chuckled. "My, you are a beginner, aren't you?" He studied the board and made an advance. "You know it's interesting what's happened to the neighborhood in The Heights. It's practically unrecognizable."

"What do you mean?" I asked and made another rookie play.

"Our little circle isn't quite the same. Aren't you going to eat breakfast?"

Since he was surveying the board, I gave in and poured the milk on my Cheerios, noticing the fancy ceramic pitcher. I held it up. "This is new. It's pretty. I usually get my milk from one of those little cartons, like in grade school. Did you go yet?"

"No, I'm still thinking. Please eat."

After a couple of bites, Lance took his turn and I made my move, purposely leaving my Queen open so we could end this back and forth.

Lance cleared his throat. "So, as I was saying, everything in the neighborhood changed, you know, once you showed up. It was a peaceful, happy place until then."

In an effort to get him to stop going down this road, I pretended I didn't hear him and ate some more cereal.

My head dizzied and I shook it off. "You know, I'm not feeling so great. Maybe we could finish this game another time."

He advanced toward my queen. "But I have a lot to say right now. It's your move."

A heaviness fell over me and it was all I could do to make another terrible play.

Check me and get out, Lance Anderson!

"It's… uh… it's your turn," I slurred.

"Yes, it is. You've caused me a world of trouble, did you know that? I had it pretty good before Annabelle Wright went to Wine Down Wednesday and met my wife. Actually, we all did. Now, look at us. Nicole is dead. My friend, Dave, is in jail. Catherine and Mick are getting divorced, and Wendy found out about my mistress, Julie."

I could barely keep my eyes open. "I didn't have anything to do with any of that."

"But you did tell my wife I was cheating on her with her best friend. She tracks me with some app you told her about. My life has become a living hell. I had my cake and was eating it too. You blew up my life. What do you have to say for yourself?"

The room spun as I fell back on my pillow, unable to form a sentence. I heard Lance shift on the bed and then his face was right next to mine. "Don't fight it, Anna. This is your payback for fucking me over."

The milk. Lance poisoned me. I didn't fight it. I wanted to slip away and be free.

I'm coming, Jack.

As I took my final breaths, I asked for God's forgiveness.

The last thing I remembered was Lance whispering in my ear, "Checkmate."

THE END

ACKNOWLEDGEMENTS

AS ALWAYS, I WANT TO thank my two Bs, Bill and Brownie. My husband and my senior rescue dog are the sweet peas of my life. I'm so lucky I get to grow old with both of you. Thank you for your support, morning cuddles with coffee, and letting me sleep in when my mind has been spinning all night long. I love you.

To Kate Miles, my partner, my sounding board, and dear friend. Thank you for being there when I want to give up. You're always there to tell me to keep my chin up. It's been quite the JOURNEY, because you always say, "Don't Stop Believing." (See what I did there?)

To my beta and proofreaders, Katy Corbeil, Vanessa Spinner, and Sally Gillespie, thank you all so much! I appreciate you treating this book baby like one of your own and making it better. You are all wonderful, beautiful friends. I adore you!

To Debbie Watson who does the heavy promo lifting each and every day. You are a machine and I appreciate you so much.

To Lainey Da Silva from DS Book Promotions and all of your amazing bloggers. Oh, my goodness! Thank you so much. Your attention to detail and kindness are second to none. You rock!

To the admins of the large book groups on Facebook, thank you for volunteering your time so small authors like me have a chance to connect with more readers. I'm sure some days it's very frustrating, but I see you. I appreciate you.

To the members of my small reader group on Facebook, thanks for being there for me. I know I'm not the most active author on social media and I tend to keep to myself, but I'm grateful to each and every one of you.

To my family and friends that continue to support my dream, you mean the world to me. I know I'm kind of the weird one that doesn't socialize much and posts a lot of goofy memes, so just know you are special to me.

And to my hometown, Waynesboro, Pennsylvania, thanks for helping out this former graduate by embracing the Hope Ridge series. I hope to meet you all in person. I'd love to do a signing in Waynesboro someday. Perhaps I'll set up a card table next to FAT Russ' BBQ food truck and go to town signing books and eating macaroni and cheese!

ALSO, BY ROSEMARY WILLHIDE

Swept Away series:
Running Away to Home
Away with Him
A Way Back
Swept Away Box Set
Derek's Christmas Carol: A Swept Away Special Edition

Vegas Edge series:
Temptation
Desire
Fury
Vegas Edge: Box Set

A Hope Ridge Mystery series:
Killer Fiction – Book One
Killer Deception – Book Two
Killer Revenge – Book Three

Standalone stories:
Power Play: Go Big or Go Home!

AUTHOR BIOGRAPHY

I'M AN ACTRESS, TURNED FITNESS instructor, turned author. I've told stories and entertained people my entire life. Writing is my favorite because I don't have to leave the house or put on pants. Plus, the voices in my head always do what I say, for the most part. LOL!

I live in Las Vegas with my husband, Bill, and my adopted pooch, Brownie. I still teach cycling classes. It keeps me sane-ish.

Welcome to my world.

ROSEMARY WILLHIDE

Printed In Great Britain
by Amazon

37066151R00148